PRAISE

NINE D...

"My mom is 91, and this wonderful book helped me to think about, cry about and prepare for the inevitable. It also made me think of my own life and how I want to live it as though it were my last. There were so many scenes I loved. I could see and smell them."

　　– Rachel Nicholas, Recording Artist

"Judy Lannon's creative approach brings the reader into Sara's world of wit, sarcasm, self-doubt, courage, strength and love. The mixed amounts of humor and heaviness in the story truly brings it home."

　　– Terece Horton, Author of *Rebecca's Gift*

"Judy Lannon invites the reader into the mind and heart of Sara, the daughter of a narcissist mother. This complex character comes to life with every page as we witness her transformation from needing external validation to discovering the values within herself."

　　– Mary Obana, Author of *Shine: A Simple Guide to Finding Your Light and Letting it Shine on the World*

"I connected with Sara. She is real; frustrated in her job, questioning herself and some of her life choices and has family drama. Readers will relate to at least one if not all these topics. Many of us have self-doubt and can easily see ourselves in Sara's shoes. Sara isn't a perfect character and that is what I love about her. Not to mention how often have we desired an IV of vodka or anything powerful to pull us out and away from our stressful lives."

　　– Lisa Allison, AIPT Comics

NINE DAYS

JUDY LANNON

atmosphere press

To all mothers who raise strong daughters and all daughters who are raised by strong mothers

PREFACE

This story is fictional, as are the Austin family, relatives, friends, colleagues, healthcare workers, and anyone else who may have popped into it. However, even though these characters are fictional, we might recognize that they may have similar traits to people that we actually know. People that we might love, or hate, or could care less about, but people who have crossed our path in life. We might even recognize some of these traits in ourselves, good and bad.

My grandmother told me about Sara. Even though she left this earth over twenty years ago, I know that she is always with me in spirit. My grandmother often comes to me when she feels the time is right. There was one particular night that she came to me in a dream and told me that I would meet Sara. She told me to be on the lookout for her. I wasn't sure how I would meet Sara. However, even from eternity, I listen to what my grandmother has to say.

It is Sara who inspired me to write this story. I have never met Sara in person. She is woven into my imagination. Sara is an enigma.

Peace to her soul; French condolence.
May she rest in heavenly light; Turkish condolence.
May her memory be a blessing; Jewish condolence.
May you live to remember her; Greek condolence.
May her spirit remain in your life; Egyptian condolence.

THURSDAY

"Do not dwell in the past, do not dream of the future,
concentrate the mind on the present moment."
– Buddha

I t's February and I am sitting on one of the many amazing terraces at the Ocean Club Bahamas resort, taking just a few minutes to let the warm sun shine on my face and to breathe in the sight of the sparkling blue-green water to soothe my anxiety. I made sure to apply sunscreen to my face; I already have too many brown spots as it is. My long dress isn't necessarily for sun protection, more to protect my poor body image.

I wish I was on vacation but I'm here to oversee a conference for two hundred of my colleagues, which I have spent months coordinating. This, by the way, is not in my job description. I actually don't even have a job description and I have no experience in event planning. But I did it, and I think I've done a good job. I found the venue, negotiated a palatable rate. I worked my ass off to book two hundred guest rooms, secured small conference rooms for the various training sessions that will be held. I managed the different menus for the catered events, organized the shipping, sent out invitations, decided on the lighting, music, DJs; the list is endless. But I'm here, with fingers crossed and a somewhat shaky positive attitude.

Earlier today, I gave my dogs hugs and pats; no pats for my husband, Keith—instead he got a hug, and a kiss. I got in my car and took the miserable two-hour drive from my home in Newport, Rhode Island to Logan Airport. This gave me plenty of time to reflect—stew, actually—on this week. Damn is all I have to say, damn it's been a hell of a week, and it's only Thursday.

The week started on a great note; our team, the Patriots, won the Super Bowl. Monday morning that sweet victory was forgotten when Keith woke me up to tell me he just got an upsetting phone call; his best friend from childhood, the best man at our wedding, died in his sleep the night before.

"They think it was a heart attack," he said.

"Jesus, Keith, Bob's so young. What's going to happen to his kids?" This is so unsettling. Bob is younger than me, I think he was fifty-nine. He seemed healthy, but I guess we just don't know what's around the corner for any of us.

"No idea. I mean, they must still be dealing with losing their mother last year. Even though they're in their twenties, this has got to be horrible. Both parents gone within a year of each other," he said before walking out of the bedroom, head down, shoulders slumped. His posture spoke volumes of what Keith couldn't or didn't want to articulate.

After I processed the news of Bob's death, I had a second cup of coffee and sat down to work. It didn't take me too long before I realized I was struggling to focus on my long list of to-dos for the week. I work from home, so the commute from bedroom to home office is a fairly easy one. I guess you could say I wasn't on my game at all. I emailed my supervisor, Brett Prentice, who just happens to be the CEO of the marketing firm I work for. I told him what I was dealing with: an unexpected death. I probably shouldn't be working, but wanted to let him know what was going on in my life right now. I was hoping he would tell me to take the day off. No response, which wasn't like him. The work kept piling up; people were hounding me. Sara, you need to add to our room count, Sara, I want, Sara do this. Everyone wanted an immediate response from me. I was drowning, all of the pressure adding to my stress and my already borderline high blood pressure.

Monday and Tuesday were pretty much a blur of activity for me. I did my best to keep up with the last-minute planning and changes for the conference and I knew that I needed to make sure nothing went wrong. I knew that I needed help.

"Hello, Ocean Club, how may I direct your call?"

"Rebecca Sterling, please."

"Let me connect you, one moment please."

"Hello, this is Rebecca Sterling."

"Rebecca, Sara Austin here, how are you?"

"Hi Sara, I'm doing well, how are you doing? I was just going over your contract and finalizing the last-minute details for your event."

"I'm just fine, other than more last-minute revisions to the original contract."

I went over my long list of changes with Rebecca.

"I can take care of this. I had added in extra rooms to your count when we first started the paperwork. So there is absolutely no issue to increase those numbers. But I do need to alert the catering manager immediately about the meal count increasing. Just send me the list of names for the additional rooms, their guests, any food allergies, and the names of the people who have requested special meals. Basically, everything you did for the first round of reservations. I'll rework the training room's layout to make sure we can fit more chairs in without overcrowding. Is there anything else I can help with?"

"Just one more thing. Brett has taken on a new admin, who has been helping me out with some of the logistics. Just in case something gets missed or overlooked, can you please copy her on any emails going forward? Her name is Lexi Hanson. I'll send you her contact information. I think that should take care of everything—famous last words, right? At some point I need to tell people it's too late to make changes. I think we've already reached that point. I'm just going to turn off my phone, no calls, no texts, shut down my email, turn off messaging. Anything to stop being interrupted and actually get some work done," I say sarcastically. "But seriously, thank you, you are a lifesaver. See you in a couple of days." I sit back and take a sip of coffee, thinking about Lexi Hanson. She's been with the company for about six months, and it was only recently that Brett had her reach out to me to see how she could help out with the conference. I'm not sure what my take is on Lexi. Is she an asset or a threat to my position? We've only met on Zoom calls, so I'm not sure if I can make a good judgment call on her character. I usually go with my gut, and my gut is saying to observe Lexi Hanson quietly.

Now all I needed to do was keep from cracking, but I still had to deal with all of my other responsibilities and meet some unreasonable deadlines the marketing team was putting on me. Typically, I like being busy; I don't mind putting in the extra hours—I like a challenge—but the excessive demands were just about more than I could handle.

Wednesday was when the email arrived from Brett Prentice.

Sara, I understand you have some personal issues going on, but it has been brought to my attention that you are not delivering the quality of work that I expect from you. I have been told that you are not responding to requests in a timely manner, which has negative outcomes across the firm. People need to rely on you, but lately this doesn't seem to be the case. Let me know when you arrive at the resort, we can meet to discuss. Brett

I wanted to vomit. I don't take criticism well; I took this personally and it ate away at what little confidence I had. *You need a thicker skin, Sara.* I have heard this my entire life.

This is why, despite sitting in the sun at this spectacular resort, my stress level is at an all-time high.

"Hello?"

"Hi, it's me, Jessica."

"I know. I have caller ID."

"Don't be a jerk, Sara. Why do you always need to be so difficult?"

Deep breath. I try to take a deep breath, with shallow results. Did Jessica just feel like calling out of the blue to tell me that I'm difficult?

"Genevieve is sick."

"What do you mean, she's sick? How sick is she?"

"She went to the hospital. By ambulance."

"Shit, she went by ambulance? What happened?"

I listen while my older sister fills me in on the details. Our ninety-four-year-old firecracker of a mother, Genevieve Austin, would not be caught dead in an ambulance. Poor choice of words, I think. According to Jessica, our mother had started vomiting thick black fluids this morning. Genevieve's part-time aide, Kathy, was there, which is probably the only reason she even got to the hospital. Thank god for Kathy. Otherwise, Genevieve would be home alone. Who knows what might have happened?

SHIT, SHIT, SHIT. This timing sucks. Can I just disappear, pretend the plane never arrived in the Bahamas?

I had arrived at the resort a couple of hours ago. It is a vacation paradise, but my day planner shows that I'm scheduled in an hour to do a walkthrough with Rebecca and Lexi to sign off on all the menus. Thirty minutes after that I have a meeting with the training coordinator to sign off on each room setup for the trainings, discuss and approve lighting and audio with the AV team, and then meet with my boss to discuss whatever it is that he feels he needs to tell me about my obvious shortcomings. I had put Brett in as a high priority for today, even though all the other stuff going on is what will make this conference run smoothly. Meeting with him only adds an element of unnecessary anxiety. I'm pretty sure he is going to say, "What is wrong with you?"

Maybe my response should be, "Where would you like me to start, Brett? I think this meeting is causing about ninety percent of my stress. The conference, I'll say about five percent, and I'll give my mother's untimely illness the other five percent."

Brett is typically a fair, standup guy. Unfortunately, yesterday's email had made it clear—extremely clear—that he isn't happy with me.

Jessica is still talking. "I can't do anything because you're her healthcare proxy and I live on the other side of the country." Jessica and Genevieve have managed to put an entire country between them.

"Why didn't she call me? Should I come home?" I ask, praying, *say no, say no, please say no.* I could lose my job if I come home.

"No, don't come home. Genevieve doesn't want to worry you while you're working. I'll keep you posted. She'll take my calls. I'll call you later. Bye."

Jessica has always been the sky-is-falling kind of control freak.

Time to call Brett's cell to see when he wants to meet.

I'm sitting on one side of one of the many Olympic-sized swimming pools, and I can see Brett on the other side of the pool. He is sitting in a lounge chair drinking a beer with a few of the elite members of his marketing team, buckets of beer on ice for all. I see him look down at his cell—call from Sara, I am sure I'm on his caller ID. I watch him take a gulp of beer and pick up the phone. I have planted myself behind a palm tree with my sunglasses on so I can watch him as we talk, and hope that he doesn't spot me.

"Hi, Brett. I'm here. I checked in a little while ago, so just letting you know that I've arrived. This place is pretty amazing." I am trying to sound upbeat, confident, and laid back, all at the same time.

"Oh, hi Sara. Good that you're here. Everything okay? Nothing that I need to do, no fires for me to put out, I hope." He takes another gulp of beer.

I give a fake laugh."No fires, everything is good. But you said you wanted to meet with me when I got here. So here I am. I have some time later this afternoon, if that works for you." Ugh, I want to vomit—not like Genevieve, but my stomach is churning.

"Oh, that's right. Look, I don't think that this is the time or the place to discuss my concerns. Put something on my calendar, say thirty minutes. It's important that we sit down and talk. I'm traveling for the next couple of weeks, so let's try for the end of the month. But in the meantime, I need you to triple-check everything you do. Oh, and invite Henry to that meeting. It will be good to have a partner's take on the situation."

I watch Brett take another sip of his beer and readjust his backward baseball cap. I can tell by his body language that Sara Austin is the last thing he wants to deal with. He wants sun, fun, and beer, not me, so I just act like this is all normal. I just act like it is totally normal to spend days agonizing over that stupid email he sent and which now he doesn't want to talk about. Instead, I now have to wait another three weeks to find out what I have done to warrant this kind of attention from the CEO.

"Oh, okay. I'll take a look at your calendar and schedule something. Bye." I just hang up. I'm sure that anyone else would have pushed him for some kind of an explanation, but this is what I do. I act like nothing bothers me. It's so much easier to pretend everything is simply fine than to actually look reality in the face.

I sit observing Brett. I wish I could read his mind. What did he think of the call? Probably nothing. I'm sure the beers are mellowing him out, or clouding his memory, but

I know that I need to figure out what I've done. Why am I on Brett's radar, and not in a good way? I barely had any contact with him earlier in the week. I have no idea why he sent that email. What does Henry have to do with this? This makes no sense and it's not going to for weeks. This can't be about the mix-up with the PowerPoint slides that happened weeks ago. I am sure that got resolved. During a potential client presentation, a slide for another client was included and the blame landed on me. I said that I didn't do it, and I couldn't offer an explanation of what happened. I could have said someone in marketing did it, but I didn't do that. I could have advocated for myself but I didn't do that either. I just hoped it would go away with my weak *"I didn't do it, I don't know how that could have happened."*

I take a breath, hoping that, just this once, I could get some freaking air in my lungs. I put my mother on the back burner. Time to start checking off some stuff on my ridiculously long to-do list. A little secret: I love to make lists and check stuff off. I am also really good at putting my mother on the back burner.

FRIDAY

> "So, we beat on, boats against the current,
> borne back ceaselessly into the past."
> – F. Scott Fitzgerald

"**H**ello?"

"Sara, it's me, Jess."

"I know. I still have caller ID."

"Don't be such a freaking jerk, Sara. They put a tube down Mom's nose. She's horrible and I'm worried." Jessica sounds annoyed and concerned. And I guess that I have now graduated from difficult to a freaking jerk.

"Sara, I know you're working, I know that you're under a lot of stress and that you are extraordinarily busy, but I'm really uneasy about Mom." Jessica sounds anxious, a note of worry in her voice that I've never heard before.

"What do the doctors have to say? She doesn't still have that idiot Masterson, does she?" I am concerned, but I also don't like that my martini is getting warm. That idiot Masterson is Genevieve's primary care doctor. We have all been trying to convince her to fire him and find someone else.

"I'm pretty sure Masterson doesn't have hospital privileges, thank god. But it doesn't matter since they won't talk to me anyway, only you or Genevieve, and she can't talk because of the tube."

"Jesus Christ, so we have no idea what's going on with her?" I just want someone to make this all go away, please.

While Jess talks about all that could go wrong, that Genevieve is alone, nobody there to advocate for her, not knowing what is going on, I take the last sip of my martini and look at my to-do list. Time to put my personal life away, again, and get back to work. It never once occurred to me that I should call Genevieve or the hospital to find out who is treating her and what the hell is going on. I guess I won't be receiving the Healthcare Proxy of the Year award this year.

Genevieve is the matriarch of the Austin family. There are four of us: Jessica, me, Parker, and Raymond, then four grandchildren and four great-grandchildren. Genevieve isn't a warm, nurturing mother—quite the opposite—but she "did the best she could do," as she so often reminds all of us.

Our father, Michael Austin, was a handsome, charming alcoholic who Genevieve divorced when we were young. Jess was twelve, I was nine, Parker six, and Ray two. We all adored our father. Mom was the disciplinarian, Dad was fun. He died a few years ago, completely estranged from all of us.

When our parents divorced it was like a tsunami tore through the family. Some of us drowned, some of us clung to life rafts, and some of us drifted away.

Jessica didn't drown. She clung to her life raft and made sure that she got to where she should be, on land with solid footing. Because she is the oldest, she has the clearest memories of life before the tsunami. My sister remembers family spaghetti dinners, Sunday morning pancakes, endless days on the beach, marching in the Fourth of July parade, Christmas mornings. But there are other memories. Our mother's anger and frustration, her lack of patience with us. Our parents weren't living together before the divorce. That didn't seem unusual to Jess. Dad would disappear for weeks at a time without any explanation about where he was. He was just gone, and after a while, we all stopped asking questions. He was an alcoholic, not someone you could depend on to be sober or to even show up. Despite this, Genevieve would occasionally go away on long weekends, letting him come and stay with us. She was still young, newly divorced, with four kids to deal with. Much too young and energetic to just give up. Genevieve felt it was in her best interest to get away, regroup, and take care of herself because nobody else would.

When Jess was about fourteen years old, Genevieve was away for a few days and Dad was staying with us. Jess came to my elementary school at the end of the school day to walk Parker and me home. I remember thinking at the time, *This is weird, Parker and I always walk home alone, we don't need her, and why isn't she in school? How come she didn't have to go today but Parker and I did?*

Jess told us we were going to pick up Ray at his babysitter's house; she said that Dad was sick, so he couldn't be the one to get Ray. "That is the story. Dad is sick," Jess had said. "We need to stick to our story, and we are never, ever to tell Genevieve."

The three of us walked together to the babysitter's house, lied to the lady who took care of him, said our dad was sick, and we were taking Ray home. We stuck to our story. Jess put Ray in his stroller, and she told us about her day as we all walked home together. Jess had skipped school to make sure Dad didn't leave the house. He told her that since she had decided not to go to school, they should have a picnic at the beach. Jess told him it was too cold for the beach, but he told her to get a sweatshirt and find the cooler. Jess did as she was told and watched as he put the cooler in the trunk of the car. They drove to the market, got pre-made sandwiches with potato chips, soda, and cookies. The next stop was a liquor store. Jess waited in the car. She watched as Dad came out with a case of beer and two bags of ice, heard him load the cooler with ice and beer, lots of beer. I'm positive that he didn't tell Jess that his plan was to drink most of the day away, but somehow my sister knew something wasn't right. And why he decided it was okay to bring his daughter along on this binge is a mystery to all of us. Well, to all of us that know the story. What is surprising is that none of us were shocked by any of this. No one ever told us that our father was an alcoholic. No one explained to us why we had a father who was hell-bent on getting drunk. No one ever told us anything that would appear distasteful.

That was the day Jessica Austin taught herself how to drive. She helped him lug the heavy cooler down to the beach, spread out a big blanket, and ate her sandwich. He didn't eat, just kept drinking can after can of beer disguised in a paper cup. She listened to him go on and on about how unfair his life was, and with each can of beer, he became more inebriated. Dad was drunk. How would they get home safely? Jess was just a kid when she put him in the back seat of the big Chrysler, slid behind the steering wheel, put the column lever into drive, and drove her drunk father home.

Somehow, she had taken over. Jessica was in charge. This is how my sister approaches her life. Take charge, be perfect, work hard, and you will reap the rewards. Jess is twenty-five years into her second marriage and life is finally working according to plan. She has a great relationship with her two adult children, who, like their mother, are extraordinarily successful professionals. Jess retired last year, which gives her time to volunteer, reading to young migrant kids, hoping to give them a better start in life. She and her husband Russ love to travel, enjoy fine wines, and try out new recipes. Russ golfs and reads three papers a day. Jess goes to Pilates and reads four papers a day. There are plenty of days when I want to be Jessica Austin.

Parker survived the tsunami by following Jessica's example and grabbed his own life raft. Like Jess, his raft was a bit flimsy and neither of them were protected from the storms. Despite a challenging childhood, Parker became a well-known, extremely successful entrepreneur. There may be doubts about which sibling had it the worst in this family, but Parker is a strong contender for first place. As a child, it was confusing to him when our parents actually divorced. He didn't quite get what the big deal was. Dad was rarely around anyway, and our mother was still an unreasonably difficult person. However, Parker, like Jess and me, does remember warm times, snuggling on the couch with our father and Jess and me, listening to him tell us stories he would make up to keep us entertained. Ray was tiny then, off to the side in a bassinette. Parker has other memories that are stronger and much less comforting. Memories of being dropped off at a bus station to wait for Dad to meet him so they could spend the day in the city. Which one of our parents thought it was a good idea for a kid to wait alone at a bus station? Memories of Dad not showing up, memories of fear, abandonment, shame. Just like the rest of us, Parker received no motherly support from Genevieve for most of his childhood. *Buck up, Parker.* And buck up Parker did. He is also charming and handsome, like our father, but there is a big difference in how father and son turned out. In college, my brother learned how to network and how to make people feel comfortable. People trust Parker. After graduating from Brown University, Parker started his own small tech company, which he turned into a "company to watch" and sold three years after inception. He has since moved on to developing several other cutting-edge companies. Parker hires just the right people to guarantee success and then he sells the businesses at phenomenal profits. He works extremely hard to prove to the world that he is someone that can be depended on; he will be there when he says he will. Parker Austin strives to never disappoint.

As for me, I simply drifted away. There are times that I will come in with the tide for a while, maybe out of necessity, but I have always made sure to hop onto an outgoing tide more often than the family likes. I guess you could say I don't have many of the same traits as Jess and Parker. I am aloof, sensitive, and highly protective of myself. Once our father left the family for real, I basically shut myself off emotionally to avoid any chance of hurt feelings and conflicts. I remember as a child that I never spoke up for myself, which I hated about myself. I learned at a young age that being in the shadows, staying quiet, and staying out of the limelight let me fly under the radar. I avoided confrontations. I would go along with what was being said or told to me. Parker and Jessica always spoke up and didn't care how much they drove Genevieve crazy.

I lived in a bubble that I created for myself. I preferred animals to people—still do. Animals offer no judgment, no criticism, just unconditional love. I started riding horses at a young age and learned, surprisingly from Genevieve, that a horse responds better to a gentle hand on the reins, and that if pulled on or tugged, the horse would resist. I think that I approached my life this way, although it wasn't a conscious decision. I sometimes wonder if this gentle side of me made me a target for the family. Genevieve often told me that I had no backbone, that I was like a jellyfish, wishy-washy. When I was in the second grade, the class read a story about trees. The one part that has stayed with me about that little book is how a tree needs a strong trunk and strong roots to be able to bend with the wind without toppling over. I was like that growing up. I was like a young tree, trying to grow a strong trunk, trying to plant roots, desperately trying not to topple over.

Raymond, "Ray," the youngest of us Austin kids, drowned psychologically and he isn't even aware of it. Ray is just like our father—at least that is what he's been told. Ray says he doesn't remember Dad, other than a gray memory here or there. To add insult to injury, there are very few photos of Ray as a baby, as if he wasn't a part of our family. My youngest brother is also a handsome young man who drinks too much, loves partying and drugs, and is as inaccessible as Dad was. We call him Sting Ray, for the cutting sarcasm that he freely hurls when you are talking with him. Ray carried one trait of our mother's that he hated in her and should have hated in himself. Their words to others can be so cutting, so sharp. They are experts at knocking people down. If someone's feelings are hurt by ideas or opinions that differ from them, so be it.

"You liked that book? You are insane, that is the worst book ever published, a complete waste of my time. I told them that when I returned it to Barnes and Noble. Raymond, you have absolutely no brains when it comes to knowing the difference between literature and garbage." Those are our mother's actual words about a book that Ray had enjoyed and made the mistake of telling her about. Instead of seeing this behavior as hurtful, Ray voiced his opinions the same way she did. To him, to us, this is normal behavior. Somewhere along my crazy life, I made a deliberate choice to not carry on that trait. And during the times that I catch myself being like Genevieve, sounding harsh, letting my words cut someone down, I try to catch myself and change course. I try to be better than that. I try to be better than my mother.

Another nickname we have for him is "Stay Away Ray." I believe that for the longest time, Ray felt like an outsider, not sure where he belonged in this family. Ray tried, or at least he thought he tried, to fit in. He would call Genevieve on occasion, maybe show up for holidays, or not. I do know that for Ray, growing up, he felt inadequate compared to Jess and Parker. They are a lot to compete with. Genevieve wasn't emotionally available to her youngest son any more than she was to the rest of us.

The divorce tsunami seemed to have little effect on Genevieve, as if she were out of town when it hit our family. While we were all reeling, struggling for air and land, she remained independent, strong, defiant, unyielding, offering no aid to her children. "Let the world be damned" was her mantra. She had done everything right and look where that landed her. She had married when you were supposed to get married, maybe a bit younger than some of her friends, but there were extenuating circumstances. Her husband was going off to war, that was the world, the times Genevieve lived in. She worked as a receptionist, rented an apartment in Boston, and began her newly married life in somewhat of an independent way. When Michael returned from overseas, he was a different man. Oh, sure, still handsome, charming, but now there was a darker side to him. Others didn't seem to notice, but she did. Michael was drinking more than she liked, was getting drunk too often. Genevieve loved her cocktails, but she never got drunk.

Finally, after fourteen years of marriage, four kids, and countless instances of her husband's drunken disappearances, she said enough is enough. It was the early sixties; divorce wasn't a common occurrence then, but Genevieve was anything but conventional. She stood up to her parents, defied the social sting of divorce, and went back to work. None of this was easy for Genevieve, but she had the four of us to take care of, had to keep a roof over our heads, make sure there was food in the house. Fortunately for all of us—Genevieve included—her mother, our grandmother Meme, helped Genevieve to keep going and to move forward, which included taking care of us kids. Meme was our anchor. It was Meme who was there when we were little to make sure we got home safe from school and always gave us homemade after-school snacks. She was the one who filled our refrigerator, washed and ironed our clothes. But she gave us so much more than that.

Meme provided us with a solid foundation, something our parents were incapable of doing.

Genevieve started working in a wallpaper store, offering advice, for the most part, to women on what wallpaper to choose that would work well in their homes. She would go to their homes to measure the room and that would often lead to a discussion with the customer about how to decorate that room to complement the wallpaper. She gradually moved from wallpaper to high-end furniture stores. Genevieve discovered she had a passion for interior design, and she knew that she was good at it. But it was still the sixties, and as a woman, Genevieve had to fight for every client, every commission, every bit of recognition. But Genevieve being Genevieve, she came out on top. She fought through what was then a man's world and eventually opened her own home interior design studio. Clients were still calling and asking for advice up into her early nineties. Genevieve is proud of what she has done with her life, let the world be damned. Unfortunately, her kids—us—were part of that world.

Time to get back to work. I put on a hat to cover my hair, which is frizzing in the humidity, grab a breath mint to cover the smell of vodka, and head to the lobby, hoping I'll lose cell service in the elevators. I don't. Jess keeps talking as the elevator heads down from the penthouse. Yes, a sweet perk for all my hard work. Not from my company, but rather from the amazing team at the resort who are doing their best to keep my blood pressure in check and my alcohol consumption at an all-time high. I may or may not have told them that Mr. Prentice is a perfectionist and any errors, slip-ups, or oversights will fall on my head and eventually theirs.

It's been a long day, and it's only three in the afternoon. I was up early, showered and downstairs by seven a.m. to be sure the breakfast buffet was set up and to oversee the training registrations, making sure everyone was present and accounted for—no skipping out on the trainings. Then I met again with Rebecca, Lexi, and the catering team for the Saturday night dinner and confirmed that today's lunch went off without a hitch. Timing is everything and I needed to be sure all two hundred people had their lunch and were back in their classrooms before the next sessions began. They were. Brett should have no complaints.

I'm walking around the terrace surveying the setup for tonight's cocktail party with Jessica still attached to my ear. I am torn, conflicted, and so angry about this situation. I should be home, Genevieve shouldn't be sick, my sister should shut up, I shouldn't have to still be working at my age, where the fuck are my brothers?

I look up to see Brett walking towards me. "Hope that isn't bad news about tonight," he says as he walks by me, heading for the pool with a beer in his hand, still wearing his stupid backward baseball cap over his blonde hair, which is in the early stages of thinning. He's about 5'10", super skinny, and ghostly white. He's wearing a pair of Tommy Bahama swim trunks, a Ralph Lauren polo shirt, and flip-flops, which I'm sure are designer as well.

"Nope, everything is great. Don't forget your sunscreen," I say through a fake smile, hoping he doesn't catch my hint of sarcasm. Why does he have to assume that when it comes to me, he expects bad news? I start wondering what the tides are here in the Bahamas.

Jess and I hang up with the promise to keep each other

updated.

God, I hate this. Why am I still working, especially at a job that means nothing other than a substantial paycheck? *You are still working because you spent too much time having fun. You didn't plan for the future. Instead, you chose to work at a job that paid minimum wage for years. You were irresponsible for years and now you are paying the price. You will be eating cat food when you're seventy.* My inner voice, my ego, can be harsh, but it usually has a point.

I did work for minimum wage and I did it for years, but I loved what I did. I worked for a nonprofit agency that focused on helping families on the brink of either making it in life or falling to the wayside. I loved the challenge of helping them find ways to pay their bills, buy healthy groceries, apply for subsidies. To do what most of us take for granted, but they had to do it all on an unreasonably small income. Sometimes we could get creative with those obstacles. I would suggest that they use coupons, read labels, buy in bulk if something is on a good sale, so the family could cook a big meal on Sundays and then have leftovers for the week. It wasn't always fun and easy, it could be overwhelming and depressing, but I felt valued. I felt that if I could help one family get over whatever hurdles they were facing, then I did something good. I did this for fifteen years, to the point of burnout. I knew it was time for me to move on.

For the next few years, I jumped from job to job, with no direction, no motivation. Eventually, I fell into marketing with a well-known company and worked my way up the ladder. I was good at what I did, I was challenged and energized. No, I wasn't saving the world, but this job kept me preoccupied, paid the bills, and kept me from seeing what I was missing in life. I was eventually headhunted to join Brett Prentice and his small marketing team to run the creative side of the business. I jumped ship and hopped on to a new opportunity. *Mistake?* I'm not sure. The pay is good, but I feel stagnant, my creative juices drying up. What am I doing in this job that can help make the world a better place? Nothing. I am doing nothing. I am just going through the motions, doing what I am asked or told to do. Why does life depend so much on the making of money?

The Friday evening cocktail party is running smoothly, operating according to the plan I put together. We are outside on a private terrace overlooking the ocean. Soft music plays in the background, fairy lights are sparkling in the trees, and the heaters are on to take away the evening chill. Appetizers are passed precisely when I expected, six-thirty to seven-thirty. There are seven assorted food stations up and ready for business exactly one hour to the minute after the first cocktails are served. It's a beautiful evening in a beautiful location and I am not appreciating one single bit of this paradise. I walk around, smiling, mingling, making small talk, and once I am completely sure that everything is taken care of, people are eating, drinking, enjoying themselves, I quietly leave the festivities. I head to the nearest bar not associated with my group, order a double Grey Goose on the rocks, don't even bother with the olives, and head to the elevator. The doors open, I step in, the doors close, I use my special passkey and press *P* to escape from this world. The elevator takes me up fifteen floors and opens directly into my room— actually rooms, four rooms to be exact. I step out of the elevator, the door shuts, I toss my key on the hall table, kick off my sandals, walk through the penthouse, pass the kitchen with its super-fancy espresso machine and mini bar, open up the slider, and go out to my private pool overlooking the ocean. A snow moon has risen, illuminating the night sky, and the breeze seems warmer up here in my private oasis. I stand and take it all in. I breathe, really breathe. I get undressed under the stars, completely uninhibited—nobody can see me—and step into the cool water of the pool. It's saltwater. I am beyond in heaven. I dive into the water, touching the bottom with my fingertips, and then I do a perfect underwater somersault so I can sit on the bottom of the pool. I stay there, looking around, eyes wide open until my lungs force me to come up for air.

For as long as I can remember, I have fantasized about living under the ocean. The bottom of the sea is where I live. My underwater home is a sunken pirate ship, open to all since the doors and windows were lost centuries ago. My bed is a giant clamshell, in shimmery blues and greens. My blankets are layers of kelp to keep me warm when I sleep. The days are bliss as I watch over my herd of sea horses and play with the dolphins. At night, my ocean sky glows with sparkling lights courtesy of the bioluminescence. The endangered right whales come from time to time to stay with me. They want to share their ancient tales, knowing that I will be the keeper of their narratives. The great white sharks are my protectors from humans. This is where I thrive, this is where I belong, this is where I came from. It's a childhood fantasy, and it's one that I'm not willing to let go of.

I come up for air and marvel at the fact that I'm

floating on the top floor of this massive resort in my private saltwater pool. I can get used to this lifestyle, the penthouse, and all that comes with it. I'm so content, just floating along, looking at the stars and the moon, and then I hear my mother's voice. "This, Sara, this is what I have been trying to tell you your whole life. This is where you are meant to be, Sara. This is what you could have accomplished if you had applied yourself."

I dive again, as deep as possible, to the silence only being underneath the water can provide, silence my mother's voice, and savor this moment. Sometimes I wish I had listened to Genevieve, sometimes I wish she had really talked to me.

SATURDAY

"Open your eyes, look within. Are you satisfied
with the life you're living?"
– Bob Marley

I'm up early again this morning. I'm so unsettled with this Brett and Henry situation I can't seem to think of anything else. But that's not going to work if I want to pull off an amazing evening.

Coffee and a walk on the beach should help clear my head. It's early enough so I should have the beach to myself, just the way I like it.

But, as fate would have it, I run into Henry while getting my coffee. I figure it's now or never. Just do it, Sara, just talk to Henry.

"Hey there, good morning. You're up early," I say, sipping my coffee and trying to act all casual when I am actually a wreck on the inside.

"Hi, Sara. Yeah, I figured I'd get a run in before it gets too hot. It was pretty nice to run so early; the beach was basically empty. Just me and some dolphins." Henry is a pretty easygoing, straightforward guy, and I would think that if he did have issues with me, he would have come to me, not gone to Brett.

27

"Good for you. It's a beautiful place for a run. Actually, it's a beautiful place for just about anything." Deep breath. "So, I need to ask you something. Are you and I okay? I mean, are you unhappy with me? Have I done something that would make you go to Brett rather than come to me?"

Henry charges his bottled water to his room, turns around, and looks at me. "Not sure what you're talking about."

I sigh, then hope he didn't catch it. "Brett emailed me earlier in the week. He said that he was getting complaints about me. He seems concerned about me, I guess my job performance, I'm not sure. But he wants to have a meeting with you and me. I thought you might have some idea of what's going on?"

Henry looks at me, "Sara, I don't have any issues or complaints about you. I'm not sure what you're talking about. Was Brett drinking when he sent the email?"

"It was ten a.m. when he sent that email."

"So? It's always five o'clock somewhere as far as Brett's concerned. As I said, I have no complaints about you, and I'm not sure where this is coming from, other than maybe Brett is confused. I haven't talked to him about you. He hasn't talked to me about you." Henry takes a big sip of water and continues, "But right now, I need to get back to my room, shower, and change. Otherwise, I'm going to be late for my tee time."

Henry starts to walk away, but then he turns around and says, "Sara, this doesn't concern me, but you need to get it together, figure this out with Brett. Oh, and re-member that you hold the position of Managing Director. I know that Brett is difficult, but you need to act and respond in a manner that is indicative of your title. See you tonight, looking forward to a great evening."

I just stand there watching Henry walk away. What the fuck just happened? Okay, so now I am incredibly embarrassed—did I sound needy, unprofessional? Damn it, what the hell? These feelings of such angst, worry, dread seemed to be for nothing. NOTHING! For days I have been stressing over that stupid email. What the hell is going on with Brett? Why did he say those things to me? Why does he want to meet with me? Why didn't I demand that he tell me right after I got his email, why did I wait until I got here? *Because that is what you do, Sara, you avoid, you stay clear of any perceived unpleasantness for as long as possible.* Why do I not have a backbone? I have got to find another way to earn a living.

I take just a few minutes to walk out to the water's edge, get my toes in the warm white sand, and inhale the ocean air. The calm blue-green water is so different from our majestic, powerful New England ocean. Even though they seem to be polar opposites, serene versus powerful, both bring a sense of calm to me no matter what is happening around me. This is what I need to get through this time of uncertainty. I need to be powerful yet remain calm. Good luck with that, Sara.

Brett gave everyone a "Have Fun, No Workday Saturday," meaning exactly what it sounds like: have fun, don't work today. My colleagues will take full advantage of this free day, golfing, hanging out at one of the six pools, chilling at the beach, taking surfing lessons, deep-sea fishing, spa treatments—whatever they wanted to do, they were able to do. None of this applies to me. All I want to do today is hide out in my penthouse, swim in the pool, raid the mini bar, luxuriate in the amazing soaking tub, and then hit the huge walk-in shower and never leave. I want to take full advantage of every single thing in this beautiful place. I want to sit in every piece of furniture in every room, read every magazine on the coffee table. What I really want is to not have to do anything today other than enjoy and relish every square inch of all four rooms in the penthouse. Instead, I spend most of the day going over each and every last detail for tonight's event.

Finally, Saturday night, the last night of the conference. Brett told me he wanted to go all out for this evening's event, he didn't care how much I spent. So, I did it, I went all out. I did all the work; I spent his money and the outcome of all my planning and preparation is a pretty spectacular evening. Tonight's extravaganza is set on a private beach. There's a warm breeze and the sun is starting to sink low into the ocean, the full snow moon peeking out on the horizon, hinting it will be worth the wait to see it rise.

Rebecca, Lexi, and I are doing a last-minute walk-through just before the guests start to arrive.

"Sara, I hope you approve of the different island-themed floral centerpieces on each of the twenty-five tables."

"They are stunning, especially with the black linen tablecloths," I say as I look around to check that the tiki torches on the perimeter have been lit. In the background, the DJ is already spinning island tunes.

"Over here is the bar, with an assortment of local beers, a selection of wines, and only top-shelf liquor, as you requested. Do you want to try the specialty cocktail, the Gully Wash?"

"I think I'll hold off for now. I was told to be careful of

this Bahamian concoction."

"Probably a good idea. We locals call it a creeper. But don't worry, I made sure that the bartenders warn anyone who orders it."

"You think of everything," I say, smiling. I'll stick to my vodka. "The buffet is starting to look amazing." The staff is almost done bringing out all the food to feed two hundred people.

"I agree, but it's what you ordered, so take some credit for this. Lots of our island specialties, including lobsters, seared grouper, Bahama Breeze buttermilk fried chicken, conch chowder, peas and rice, assorted vegetarian platters, green salads, and porterhouse steaks. As the dinner gets under way, we'll set up the dessert table with local sweets, including almond cake, rum cake, and guava duff."

My phone rings. "I'm sorry, but I need to take this. Lexi, please finish up with Rebecca, I'll only be a few minutes."

"Enjoy your evening, Sara, it was so nice to work with you and I hope we can do this again next year."

"Hello?"

"Hi, notice I didn't say it's me, Jess. Can you talk for a minute? Are you busy?"

"I'm having dinner with two hundred of my closest friends, what's going on?" I say to Jess, but in reality, the only thing that I can deal with is for this night to go without a hitch. I wish I could kick off my sandals and let go for the evening, but tonight this is work, this is my responsibility. One lightbulb out and who knows what the repercussion might be?

"I really think Mom's dying. Sara, are you listening?"

Jess's voice brings me back to the present moment.

Back to all of the pressure and responsibilities I have, all because of this stupid dinner on the beach. I actually take a second, just one second, and look out to the ocean, checking the tide.

Why the hell can't I get a fucking deep breath?

"Yes, I'm listening. What happened?"

I'm walking around the event, trying to look normal, trying to look like everything is under control. The party is in full swing and people are starting to line up for cocktails and the buffet.

"Jess, hold on. Excuse me, sir, where are the vegetarian options I ordered?" I feel like I'm channeling Genevieve, I am pulling rank, acting superior to the Buffet Captain.

"I talked to her a little while ago, she sounds horrible."

"For god's sake, Mom has a tube up her nose, you would sound horrible, too." Sky-is-falling Jess. "Hold on again. Excuse me, but that one plate of grilled vegetables is not going to cut it, where are the platters? I ordered three large platters of assorted grilled vegetables."

I'm on overdrive—where the hell are the vegetarian options, why is my sister calling me at this very moment?

"Sara, she said she wants to die. Mom told me she wants to die. She wants them to remove the tube and just let her die."

Breathe, try to breathe, I need a deep breath. "Sir, could you please find the vegetarians and serve them from this skimpy plate of grilled vegetables? Jess, hang on." I am trying to catch a decent breath, talk to my sister, look professional, look like everything is simply perfect. I am trying to not explode in public. I am trying to not cry.

"No, I don't know where the vegetarians are sitting. Probably all over the place. You were supposed to have three large platters of assorted grilled vegetables at the buffet, not whatever that thing is that you are trying to pass off. You know what, scratch serving people from that plate you're holding. Please turn around, go back into the kitchen, and come back out with what I ordered. And try to remember, three large platters of assorted grilled vegetables, let them know this is what I ordered weeks ago, and this is what I paid for," I say in a firm, controlled tone.

Oh god, the vegetarians have formed a coalition and they're heading towards me. Jess is still talking; her voice is small.

I see an out from this crazy situation. Robert, my favorite website designer, always willing to help out, is walking towards the buffet. "Robert, hi there. I could use your help, please. There's a slight issue with the platters I ordered, specifically the veggie platters. They're going to bring more out in just a few minutes. When they do, could you please help the staff find the vegetarians? Most of them are on your team."

"Sure thing, you look like you have your hands full, I'm happy to help."

"I really appreciate you stepping in and, yes, I have a few things going on," I say with the phone still attached to my ear, still trying to look like I have everything under control. "Thanks so much."

I had made a spontaneous decision and shifted the vegetarian problem to someone else. Finally, I'm at the bar.

"Hi, vodka, rocks, lime, please—oh, and make that a double. Jess, are you still there?"

"Yup, I'm still here. I know the timing is terrible but, she really wants to die."

"Should I leave tonight?" I'm not sure why I offered—it's already nine p.m. Is there a red-eye for Logan?

"No, you're coming home tomorrow, right? I can't do anything because I'm not her proxy. I'd be there if I could be of any help. That's not a dig, just the truth of this situation."

We hang up, an air of something that I am so unfamiliar with hanging between us. Does Genevieve really want to die? That doesn't sound like her at all. I put our conversation in the part of my brain that will store it until I need it. That part is getting pretty crowded.

I stand off to the side, watching my coworkers enjoy what I put together. The dinner went according to plan, except for the disappointed vegetarians. Lots of drunk, happy people, always a good sign. I watch and listen as a buzzed Brett takes the mic and does the obligatory awards and giving-out of thank yous. He hates doing this. I know he hates putting on his CEO hat. Brett is a thirty-year-old party boy, blue-blood, prep-school, big-man-on-campus type of guy. Single and not looking for anything or anyone who will try to hold him back or tie him down. He's also a bit stunned at how successful his startup company is, making a name for itself, making him grow up, tying him down.

"There is just one other person I would like to recognize, someone who isn't a part of our market research team, which, by the way, has taken all the awards," he says with a slight slur and a definite sway to his body. There is laughter from his admirers; they all love Brett, or at least pretend to.

"You wouldn't be here if it wasn't for this one person, who, in just a short time, has contributed so much to our firm. She pulled all of this together. She's the reason that you're enjoying this great food, this beautiful resort, oh, and she also made sure you have a chair to sit on tonight, so nobody has to sit in the sand," he slurs. "Please give a round of applause for Lexi Hanson. Lexi, where are you, come on up here, honey."

Are you fucking kidding me, are you fucking joking? Lexi, my assistant for this project? I am the one who told her what to do and I am the one who made sure that she did it and did it correctly. Lexi shipped the training materials and some company giveaways to the resort. Big deal. I am the one who called to confirm the boxes had arrived. I am the one who made sure they were stored in a safe place until we needed to use them, not Lexi. I am the one who pulled this entire fucking conference together, not Lexi Hanson. This is just unbelievable. For the second time today, I am humiliated.

In typical Sara Austin fashion, I say nothing, bring no attention to myself. Instead, I smile and clap for Lexi as she goes up, all smiles. Brett hands her the microphone and pretty, young Lexi says, "This is such a surprise. Thank you so much, Brett, for giving me the opportunity to, well, to work with such an amazing bunch of talented people, but even more, thank you for believing in me and letting me show you what I can do to help the firm. Thanks again!" Lexi hands the mic back to Brett and gives him a big hug. That's when I head to the bar to order another double vodka. If I had more nerve, I'd order a triple.

Once I see that the evening events are winding down, the buffet is being cleared, the coffee and tea station is operating, I quietly disappear and go up to my room to pack for an early flight out the next morning. I cannot wait to get out of paradise. But before I go to bed, I take one more swim in my pool to attempt to center myself and soothe what little self-esteem I might still have.

SUNDAY

"I'm ready to accept the challenge. I'm coming home."
– LeBron James

My flight landed a few minutes early—that's one good thing that has happened today—and now I'm driving out of Boston heading to Newport Hospital. The traffic is awful, especially for a Sunday, which gives me time to call with Jess.

"Have you talked to Genevieve today?"

"I tried early this morning, but she's still struggling to talk with the tube."

"So, what's the tube for, what's the diagnosis?" Regardless of the Boston traffic, I'm feeling a bit more like myself. Obviously, I don't do well in paradise.

"I still don't know; you should be able to find out something when you get there. Drive careful, I'm sure you're exhausted. Call me when you know more, okay?"

I need to call Keith to let him know I survived the trip, at least physically. I'm still reeling from not being recognized at last night's dinner, or more so for not being recognized for putting together the entire fucking conference. Once again, I hear Genevieve's voice, *You need to have a thicker skin, Sara.* For god's sake, how thick does my skin need to be, as thick as a dolphin's, shark's, killer whale's? I'm not sure.

"Hi, baby, you okay, where are you?"

"Hey, honey. Yes, I'm okay. I survived, although now I am stuck in Boston traffic. Welcome back to reality, I guess. Anyway, I just wanted to let you know all is good and now I'm on my way to the hospital, so don't wait for dinner, just in case you are thinking about making dinner. I love you. I can't wait to get home." I had already called Keith this morning while waiting to board my flight and told him as much as I knew about Genevieve, which wasn't much.

As I cross over the Newport Bridge, I take in the beauty of Narragansett Bay and feel my blood pressure come down a few degrees. I am back on my island, Aquidneck Island. This is my home, this is where I live, this is where I pretend I can breathe. I have plenty of time on the drive to the hospital to think about Keith, me, us.

We have been through a lot. I think about when we first met. This makes me smile. When was the last time I smiled? A real smile, not one of my fake smiles that I seem to have perfected over the last couple of days.

My coworkers and some mutual friends of Keith's had a party. Somebody knew somebody who knew somebody at the party—our island is small. We were introduced to each other and we flirted just a bit, but it was more of a friendly kind of interaction, nothing romantic, no sparks at that moment. But Keith was the only person that I spent any time with at the party. We talked and laughed; he made me feel comfortable. I felt like I could be myself. Within a week he called me. He asked if I wanted to go see some cheesy Elvis impersonators at the Blues, which is a cool retro type of music venue. It was so fun, so silly, and then we started going out more, still just as friends. We went to the movies, saw lots of music, and in the nice weather had plenty of beach picnics. We had fun, he made me laugh, made me smile, and little by little he made me feel special, made me feel like there wasn't anyone in the world like me. Nobody had ever made me feel special, except for my grandmother. We talked a lot, shared our stories, the good, the bad, and the ugly. I was beginning to look at Keith differently. I was looking beyond Keith, my friend, to a Keith I might want to get to know much better.

One night, we were sitting on the beach at the end of my road. We had packed a cooler with smoked bluefish, oysters, cheese and crackers, and rosé. It was a beautiful summer night, just the two of us, sitting on a blanket, talking and drinking wine, waiting for the moon to rise. Keith told me that, when we first met, he felt I was too young to have a kid, definitely not someone he would want to get involved with. Kids were not a part of his plan. Keith is three years younger than me.

"Then what are we doing here, drinking and waiting for the moon to rise, spending time with each other, if Liza is not in the plan? I don't even know if there is a plan. Is there a plan, Keith? Why did you even start this?" I didn't want a plan, but I wanted a plan. God, I can be so exhausting. I remember getting ready to shut down. Some would say I was ready to head for the hills, but I prefer to head for the outgoing tide.

"Sara, I couldn't help myself. I remember you at that party. First, I heard a laugh, a really big laugh, then I saw where it was coming from. It was you, laughing and smiling. Your smile killed me—it still does. Your long blonde hair, and green eyes that might be just a little bit too close together, sealed the deal for me." Keith was smiling at me, looking almost worried by his honesty. "I've been cautious about taking our friendship, relationship, whatever you want to call it, any further. Can we just take it slow?"

"As long as Liza is in this, whatever we want to call it, then yes. Let's just have fun, let's just be us." I remember feeling so relieved that he didn't pressure me about anything. I didn't give the comment about my eyes a second thought. I happen to know that my eyes aren't too close together. I also happen to know that at times Keith's sense of humor can be a little too sarcastic, which is probably why we get along so well. It was a magnificent moonrise.

We continued to date and, eventually, we took our relationship to the next level and began living together. He taught Liza how to ride a bike, how to make sushi, and Liza taught him how to braid her hair. Keith was doing great for a guy who didn't have kids in his plan. We were together for about five years when out of the blue, in our kitchen, Keith got down on one knee, with Liza standing by.

"Sara Austin, I love you. I love you and all your issues, and I am grateful that you love me with all my issues, which are less than yours," he said with a nervous laugh. "Will you do me the honor of marrying me?"

I felt weird. I knew I loved him—why wouldn't we get married? But I wasn't used to this type of public display of affection, even though Liza was the only witness. In hindsight, I realize that I had never seen my parents interact as a couple. I had witnessed my father try to please Genevieve with gifts, some expensive and some romantic. She would always just open the present, look at it, and say thank you. There was never any enthusiasm, let alone a kiss, a big hug, an I love you, thank you so much, how did you know?

"Of course I'll marry you, stand up, give me a kiss, let me look at this amazing ring. Liza, are you good with this?" I could tell by the look on my daughter's face that she was in on this with Keith, which made it even more special.

And then the best boyfriend in the world picked me up, kissed me, and we slow-danced to a Chris Isaak song in the kitchen. Liza clapped and whistled. Keith whispered in my ear, "I promise to love you forever, Sara Austin. Love you, love Liza, love your crazy, fucked-up family." That was the most romantic thing I had ever heard.

It's six p.m. when I pull into the hospital parking lot. Damn, this has been a long day and the hardest part is just starting. I put the car in park and pull down the visor mirror. I prepare to see my mother, the formidable Genevieve Austin. "You look tired, maybe it's time you use one of those gazillion tubes of lipstick you never use. Maybe it's time you started using foundation, maybe it's time you actually lose some weight, do something with your hair."

I slam the mirror shut. These aren't my words, these are my mother's words, spoken over and over and over, different words, but same point. I hate how I look, hate that I'm not tall and thin like Genevieve. For god's sake, I am in my sixties and I'm still letting my mother push my buttons, still feeling so insecure around her. Yup, this looks like a perfect tide to take, I think as I walk through the hospital doors, not even bothering to try for a deep breath.

"Hi, can you please tell me what room Genevieve Austin is in?"

"Fourth floor, room 3799, follow the green line to the second set of elevators, which is through two sets of swinging doors."

Jeez, what if I were color-blind, how could I follow the green lines? What if I was on crutches? Genevieve would pass me in the hall on her way out of the hospital before I made it through the first set of swinging doors. Get a grip, Sara, get a grip, I say to myself. This place is a fucking maze, but I do as I'm told and follow the green line through swinging doors, past patient rooms, past despair, sickness, old age, sorrow. I am here. I am outside room 3799. I am trying to catch a breath.

"Hi, Mom."

"Sara, you're here."

Genevieve is sitting up in her hospital bed, attached to an intravenous pole, but otherwise looking amazing for being ill and ninety-four years old. Damn, she has good skin, I think as I lean down to give her a kiss on her cheek. That's when I notice the terrible purple bruises on her hands and arms.

"Mom, you look great—Jess made it seem like you were dying, you know, sky-is-falling Jess."

"I did want to die," Genevieve responds. "It was horrible, that tube was just terrible, I could barely talk. I made them remove it this afternoon. I didn't care what happened to me. I needed that damn thing to go. Your sister has been terribly worried, she told me she called you. I wish she hadn't."

"Well, I'm glad that she did. So, seriously, what is going on with you?"

"Oh, they don't know yet. How was your trip?" Genevieve waves her hand in the air as if to make it all go away.

"My trip was fine, but let's talk about you." Typically, my mother's favorite subject. "Why on earth are you in the hospital?"

"I haven't been feeling well for some time now. I'd say since before Christmas."

"You were great at Christmas."

Genevieve smiles. "I was faking it. I pulled myself together. I wanted it to be a wonderful Christmas."

"It was," I respond. I'm feeling uneasy. This isn't Genevieve talking, who is this woman? It was a wonderful Christmas and would go down as one of the better ones. That holiday, like all the others, is a love/hate time for me. I love the idea of the holiday, the preparation, decorating, shopping, whatever it is that would be considered a tradition for my family and me. For me, that family is my husband, daughter, and grandchildren. For years, the holidays were not a time I enjoyed being with my mother, and my father was a non-factor for most of my adult life. But it was also a time that I enjoyed being with my sister and brothers when we were younger. We had a falling-out years ago, such a tasteful way of saying there was a big fight about one of us not coming for some holiday or family dinner, and everyone stopped talking to each other. Of course, no one ever got mad if Ray was a no-show. In hindsight, years later, I think that most of us realized it wasn't about who didn't show up, it was us realizing the cracks in our family were starting to widen.

"Well," Genevieve continues, "I haven't been able to eat for days, and then on Friday, I started vomiting disgusting, vile, thick fluid. Kathy was there, she took one look at me and said, 'Genevieve, I'm taking you to the hospital.' Sara, I was too weak for her to drive me, I told her to call the ambulance."

"Damn, you must have been feeling really shitty to come in an ambulance."

"I was, and please don't use that language, Sara. You were raised better than that."

"So now what?" I am struggling to keep my feelings at bay. Even here, attached to an IV, Genevieve pushes my buttons.

"I'm not sure at this point. I've had a CT scan, more blood tests than I care to think about, some other procedure—I can't remember what that was—and that damn tube, but nobody is telling me anything."

"What's the intravenous bag for?"

"Oh, that damn thing," Genevieve says. "I'm not sure how many veins it took before they could get it in. I haven't been able to eat, so this is giving me some nutrients and fluids. Now, tell me about your trip. When did you get back?"

"I got back today and came straight here." I fill my mother in with all the highlights, the beautiful resort, the warm weather. I describe the penthouse in great detail, and leave out the struggle going on between Brett and me. I leave out how I hate my job. I leave out how I was overlooked. I leave out a lot of things. I just want to keep all of that to myself as usual.

A nurse's aide enters the room. "Good evening, Genevieve, my name is Lorna, and I am here to take your vitals." Lorna is a large, beautiful woman with a lovely Jamaican accent. My antenna is up.

"Hello, Lorna, aren't you a healthy-looking woman, and such great big brown cheeks. What nationality are you?" *Noooo*, I scream inside my head, *no, Mom, please no.* I know where this can go. How much do you weigh? Have you always been this big? What do you eat? Genevieve has no filter.

"Thank you. I am very blessed to be so healthy. My goodness, your nails are beautiful, what shade is that?"

"Siren Rose, I think that's the color. I just had them done, toes too." Genevieve shakes a foot out from under the blanket.

Hats off to Lorna. I could use some of her confidence.

Lorna finishes taking Genevieve's vitals and Genevieve doesn't mention another word about her size, her cheeks, or her accent. I can tell that she is tired, not from lack of sleep, but a different kind of tired—tired to the bone.

"Sara, what day is this?"

"It's Sunday, Mom."

I say goodnight to my mother, follow the green line in the opposite direction, get in my car, and drive home. I am also tired, drained, running on low batteries, but I need to call Jess.

"I'm just leaving Genevieve; she looks great without the tube. Back to her old self, almost insulting people who are what she would consider overweight."

"Oh dear," Jess sighs.

"Basically, I have no updates. Mom doesn't know what the diagnosis is, but I hope to find out tomorrow."

"You must be exhausted. Get some sleep and call me tomorrow."

You are right, sister of mine, I am exhausted, but I still need to call Liza, I think as Jess and I hang up.

"Hi, Mom, are you back? How was your trip, how was the resort?"

"Hi, Liza, yes, I got back a little while ago. The resort was amazing, and your old mother stayed in the penthouse! You and Sam should try to get there soon. Listen, honey, I need to tell you something." I pause. "Genevieve is sick."

"Oh no, what's wrong?"

"I'm not quite sure, but she's been in the hospital since Friday. She was vomiting so much that Kathy called an ambulance."

"Oh, it must be serious if Genevieve went by ambulance." We all know Genevieve so well, I think.

"No kidding. I just left her. She's pretty weak, not eating anything, but feels well enough to try to insult a nurse's aide."

Liza lets out a little laugh. "Well, at least she's up to that."

"I'll call you tomorrow when I have more news. Bye, Liza."

"Night, Mom."

On my way home from the hospital, I think about my conversation with Genevieve about Christmas. So many had been disasters. I've always envied families that glide through the holidays, enjoy being with each other, know where they will be year in and year out. Since Liza was a baby, I have juggled our Christmas schedule and it seemed to work. Liza, close friends, and I would celebrate Christmas together every Christmas Eve. It was festive, centered around Liza, fun times, presents—lots of presents—and good food. She would spend Christmas Day at her father's and I would usually spend the day with

Genevieve, Parker, and maybe Ray. Jess was married with a daughter and son of her own. She had started her own traditions.

Time moved on. Keith and I married. Parker got married, Liza married, Ray was Ray, traditions changed. Genevieve didn't do well with these changes; they didn't suit her. Now that there were great-grandchildren, Genevieve was no longer the center of attention. She became more difficult to deal with, at least for me. She was becoming extremely negative, and she was taking her criticism up a notch, if that was even possible. She expected everyone to dote on her. I began to dread this holiday. Parker always seems to do just fine. He loves to host Christmas; he's good at it. He's a great cook, which he learned from Meme. He makes the food that Genevieve loves, pairs just the right wine with each course. Parker and his wife Jill give gifts that are thoughtful and perfect for each of us. Jess, on the other side of the country, sends gifts and is sure to call when everyone's together. For years, Ray would use the excuse of "I called but you weren't there." Of course, that changed when everyone had cell phones, but he still uses that excuse, knowing Genevieve doesn't use her cell.

But, yes, last Christmas had been perfect. Keith, Genevieve, and I spent the morning at Liza's with her husband Sam and their kids, Tess and Max. We opened gifts, sipped mimosas, and had a wonderful brunch. Genevieve was engaging with the kids, listening to what they had to say, genuinely interested in them. Not at all the usual Genevieve that any of us are used to. After Liza's, the three of us drove back to our house for champagne, oysters, and more gifts. We had a beautiful fire and a lovely stress-free Christmas afternoon. We discussed books we were reading, ranted about the current state of our country, and just enjoyed each other's company. I think that this was a first for me, being relaxed and not on edge around my mother. By early evening, Genevieve was off to spend Christmas night with Parker, Jill, and their son Brady. Jeez, I thought, if you were faking it, Mom, you should be up for an Academy Award.

I pull into my driveway. The outside lights are on, smoke is coming out of the chimney—Keith has a fire going for me—I'm home. I let out a big sigh of relief. I am so happy to be home. Keith and the dogs come out to meet me; he grabs my luggage and I collapse in his arms. "How's Genevieve?"

"I have no idea. But she looks better than I do. I need vodka, please, and you can fill me in on what has been going on here. Any updates on arrangements for Bob?"

"I got what looked like a large group text. He's being cremated and the kids will do some type of memorial for him in the summer. They added in a few places for donations in his name. I can't believe he's really gone. I'm so glad you're home, baby," says Keith as he gives me an extra-strong hug.

DAY ONE

"Nothing in life is to be feared, it is only to be understood.
Now is the time to understand more, so that
we may fear less."
– Marie Curie

Today is like the first day of school, except it's the first day of—well, actually I'm not sure what.

I just know that this Monday morning arrived too fast. I struggle to get out of bed, check my emails with coffee in hand, then shower and do the thirty-minute drive back to the hospital. In the last twenty-four hours, I have traveled from the Bahamas to Logan Airport, driven two hours to Newport, visited my mother in the hospital, talked to my sister more than I have in the last year, unpacked, then packed again. This time I packed my work laptop, cell phone, office supplies, anything that I need to show that I am working at least eight hours today. Fortunately, my job is about seventy percent remote, so I'm sure I can pull this off. There is no way that I am going to ask for time off, let anyone from work know what is going on in my world. What's one day working out of the hospital room?

I arrive at the hospital at seven-thirty a.m., maneuver down the green line a bit better than last night, up to the fourth floor, and into room 3799. The ward is more hectic, probably because it's the morning. But there is still the feeling of unease and sadness as I pass each room. I notice there's a chalkboard outside Genevieve's room that I didn't see last night. It shows the date she was admitted and the initials N.P.O. I have no idea what that means.

"Good morning, Mom," I whisper. If only it is that, a good morning.

Genevieve is asleep even though the ward is humming with calls to the nurse's station, carts rolling by, staff talking, call buttons pressed for the third, fourth time, *please help, can someone please help?*

Her room is overlooking the harbor, with a day bed and a small desk, a perfect spot for me to set up my office for the day. I get my laptop turned on, connect to the hospital Wi-Fi, log in to my work website, and sit and wait, looking out to the harbor. So here I am, all efficient, but what am I really supposed to be doing here? I guess figure out what the hell is wrong with Genevieve and still give my all to my job. Speaking of my job, I suppose I should look at Brett and Henry's calendars to see when I should schedule the meeting for the three of us. Maybe I should title it "Meeting to discuss what is wrong with Sara."

"Sara, dear, what are you doing here?" Genevieve is awake.

"I told you I'd be back this morning, so here I am. Look, I have my work computer set up, with a lovely view. Who could ask for more?" Why do I sound so cheery and phony at the same time? "How are you feeling? Did you get any sleep?"

"God, no, they come in at all hours to wake you up to see if you're still breathing," Genevieve says as she struggles to sit up.

I go over to help her. "Jeez, Mom, you're so skinny."

"One hundred and nine pounds," she says, rather gleefully.

One hundred and nine pounds. I haven't been one hundred and nine pounds since I was eight, I think as I try to prop her up with pillows. It's then that I notice my mother's stomach. She looks like she's nine months pregnant. That's where nine of those one hundred and nine pounds are.

"Good morning, Genevieve."

We turn to see two people have walked into her room.

"Oh, and who are you?" Genevieve asks, trying to fluff her hair. I'm sure she's thinking, it's eight a.m., too damn early for visitors.

"I'm Dr. Dalton and this is Nurse Patterson. How are you feeling this morning?"

"You aren't the doctor that was here yesterday. Where is he? What was his name?" My mother does not seem pleased.

"Right, I'm not sure who that was. Amy—Nurse Patterson—and I are part of today's morning rounds team. I reviewed your case earlier and wanted to check in to see how you are feeling and if you have any questions."

"This is my daughter, Sara."

I put out my hand. "Hello, I'm also Genevieve's health-care proxy. Can you please tell us what's going on with her?"

"Well, we don't have a diagnosis just yet," Dr. Dalton says calmly.

"What about that damn tube down my nose? What did that tell you?" Ah, Genevieve is now wide awake.

I just smile at Dalton and Amy. Good luck with

Genevieve, I say to myself. She will eat you alive.

"That was a nasogastric tube, which provided you with the nutrients you were deficient in when you were admitted. We haven't received the results from Pathology for your upper GI just yet. Amy, have you seen any results on Genevieve?"

Good deflect, I think.

"No, not yet." Amy smiles rather condescendingly. My phone rings and I look down—call from Jessica. I mumble an apology, silence my phone, and try to mentally calculate what time it is in Scottsdale. Too damn early, is what I figure out.

Dr. Dalton does a brief exam of Genevieve, asks if she has had a bowel movement. Do I really need to know this, I think to myself.

"I think we should get you up and walking for just a few minutes today."

"Oh, I am much too weak to try." Again, this is not my mother. Genevieve still belongs to a gym; she shoves her boundless energy and exercise habits in everyone's face.

"Well, perhaps later today. It will do you good to get up and move," says Amy.

The two say their goodbyes without a single bit of information for either of us. Genevieve and I just look at each other.

"What the hell was that about?" I ask, more to myself than her.

"Excuse me," I say as I follow Amy and Dr. Dalton out of the room. "Can you please explain to me why Genevieve is still here? She was admitted five days ago. Why don't you know what her diagnosis is? Why is she so sick? Seriously, what have you been doing for her for these five days?"

Dr. Dalton removes his glasses and starts to clean them on his white lab coat. "Your mother was admitted with abdominal pain, vomiting, and what appeared to be acute, severe Gerd. A CT scan was performed on her abdomen with contrast. The scan showed a moderate amount of ascites as well as a small bowel obstruction."

What the hell is ascites, I wonder. At least I know that Gerd has something to do with gastro reflux. I have absolutely no idea how I know this bit of medical trivia.

"We began treating the obstruction with NPO, a nasogastric tube, which was removed at your mother's request, as well as IV fluids, and we encouraged ambulation. Your mother states she is too weak to get up and walk, even with assistance, as you just witnessed. We also consulted with Dr. Yasmin, our resident gastrologist, after the initial CT scan results were reviewed. He determined that we needed to do an upper GI endoscopy to investigate the antrum of the patient's stomach for a mass or ulceration, as well as consider paracentesis to send to cytology for her ascites. Your mother consented to that procedure, which she tolerated quite well."

"What did that show?" I ask.

"Those are the results that we are waiting for."

"Okay, back to my original question, what is Genevieve's diagnosis?" I can sense that Dalton and especially Amy feel like they have better things to do than explain all of this to me.

"Unfortunately, we don't have one yet. We know she has a bowel obstruction; we know that she has ascites, but what we don't know is the root cause of her symptoms. The endoscopy should clear this up once the biopsies are analyzed."

"When will that be?" It's like pulling teeth to get him to just tell me what I need to know.

"The results could take up to seven days."

"Seven days? That's crazy, this is already her fifth day here. Dr. Dalton, are you saying that she could be in the hospital for twelve days?" I ask incredulously, my voice rising just a bit.

"We don't like anyone to be in the hospital for that length of time. I have arranged for one of our Patient Counselors to discuss the next steps. My recommendation is for your mother to go to a rehabilitation center, where she will be monitored and get her strength back. Now, if you will excuse me, Nurse Patterson and I need to continue with our rounds. As soon as I have some information for you, I will be in touch."

I watch as they walk away, seeming all smug. I'm thinking they don't know anything, and I need to stay on top of that. Why did I agree to be her healthcare proxy in the first place?

I go back to Genevieve's room, confused by the non-answers from Dalton. I'm relieved to see that she is starting to doze off again. I find a notebook in my laptop bag and start writing down everything that I can remember of what Dr. Dalton just told me. It might as well have been in Latin. Actually, it probably is. I don't understand any of this. I need to get better, get smarter, get a grip on this situation, and I still need to work, but before I do, I need to understand what these medical terms actually mean. Thank goodness for the internet.

"Mom, I need to make a call, I'll be right back," I whisper, and head to the so-called family room, which is right down the hall. Fortunately, it's empty. I need to call Jess.

"Hey, sorry I couldn't talk when you called. Do you ever sleep?"

"No, not right now, I don't sleep right now. How is she? Have they figured out what's wrong yet?"

"We have nothing solid at this point. She's had a CT scan, the thing down her nose, and an endoscopy, which I didn't know about, but I guess she agreed to have it done. They mentioned something I had never heard of before—ascites."

"What's that?"

"It might mean that Genevieve has liver disease, but like I said, there just don't seem to be any real answers. So now we just wait for those results. Which, by the way, could take up to seven days to get the reports back from Pathology. A person could be dead in seven days."

"You mean Genevieve could be dead in seven days," Jess says.

"No, I don't mean that and actually she looks good, better than me right now, and she weighs a hundred and nine pounds. I'm not sure if that's because she isn't allowed any solid foods, which I just learned is called NPO. Why can't they just say that, no solid foods?"

"Jesus, I don't think I ever weighed a hundred and nine pounds," Jess says. "So now what? Are they talking about when she'll be discharged?"

I shrug my shoulders. "I guess we wait. We'll know more tomorrow."

"Should I come, will that help?"

"I don't know what you can do, no offense. We are going to meet with a Patient Advocate to discuss the possibility of her going to a nursing home, so she can get her strength back, still be monitored, and hopefully feel better before she goes home."

"How can she go home? They can't discharge her to just go home; she needs help, and she fires anyone we get for her. Shit, what are we going to do?" Jess is sounding panicky.

"Jess, take a breath. We are going to have to take this one day at a time, we don't know what's going on yet."

Jess is starting to raise her voice. "Sara, you aren't the one who did all the work when we tried to get Genevieve help before. There's a lot involved: interviewing agencies, trying to find the right people, setting up interviews, schedules—that all takes time, it can't be done overnight. Maybe I should come? But if I do, I can't stay indefinitely."

I'm sure my sister is having flashbacks to last summer and the disaster of trying to get Genevieve to accept home healthcare. By that time Kathy had become a part of our family. Genevieve enjoyed Kathy and Kathy genuinely cared for Genevieve. They have more of a friend relationship than a working relationship, albeit a friend that Genevieve can order around. A few years ago, Kathy had discussed increasing her hours with Genevieve, but Genevieve refused to pay her any more than she already was. "I don't need her more than an afternoon a week," she told Jessica.

It was true that, at that time, three years ago, Genevieve was doing fine on her own, for the most part. But Jess was forward-thinking. "It won't always be like this, Mom."

"Well, I don't need to worry about that yet." Case closed.

Kathy got another offer and was now restricted to just three hours a week with Genevieve. Fast-forward two years and Genevieve did need more help than three hours a week. She was depending more and more on her neighbors to run her errands, drive her to appointments, and Jess decided the time had come to find an alternative.

"Genevieve, you are taking advantage of their friendship. You need to bite the bullet and get regular weekly help."

"I will consider it when the time comes," was her answer.

That's when Jess started her own online searches for local healthcare workers. She needed to figure out what insurance would cover, if anything. And, of course, her biggest concern was if these agencies were reputable. She read online reviews, interviewed the managers of several agencies, learned the difference between a home care worker, a home health aide, and a CNA. Each has different levels of experience and responsibilities. Jess was laser-focused on Genevieve's care, much more than Parker, Ray, or me. Genevieve was coming to a point in her life when she needed more than someone to just drive her places. Jess was worried about her cooking—Genevieve was quite vocal about how often she forgot to turn the burner off on the stove—god knows she needed someone to clean, and she was starting to need help keeping her medications straight. Jess found an agency with a number of reputable CNAs and convinced Genevieve to at least interview a few people. "Who knows? Maybe you'll find another Kathy."

Parker and I agreed to sit in on the interviews when we could.

Typically, I was the one to call Jess after they were over. "It's like fucking Goldilocks, she's too fat, she's too old, she's too hard to understand." Jess would not be dissuaded from her task. "I am going to find her someone, no matter what."

Eventually, Genevieve settled on one woman, Irene, and a schedule of two mornings a week was agreed to. Jess, meanwhile, learned that the VNA would come every week to organize Genevieve's overwhelming number of daily medications for the week and take her blood pressure, all at no cost. Jess put that plan in motion as well.

A couple of weeks into this arrangement, Jess received a phone call from Genevieve. "Hi, Mom, aren't you supposed to be out with Irene now?"

"Oh, I called her, told her I didn't need her this week."

"Genevieve, you can't do that." Jess was exasperated. Genevieve was up to her old tricks.

"I don't need her, so why would I have her come? What? To just sit here? I am not paying someone to just sit here."

"You can find things for her to do. She can clean your cabinets out, do your laundry, anything. Genevieve, she is there to help you, and if you don't use her then you are going to lose her. Irene needs to make money, she needs to know who she is scheduled to work for and when, otherwise this isn't going to work."

Irene quit working for Genevieve, with the Home Agency's blessing. Genevieve went through two more aides, did the same thing that she did to Irene, and lost them as well. Jess had to call the Agency and apologize both times. They made it quite clear. Call back only when Mrs. Austin could commit to a schedule.

"Sure, Jess, you can come"—*please don't come, please don't come*—"maybe though you should wait until Genevieve goes home. Otherwise, you might just be sitting in a nursing home, doing nothing." I'm not exactly sure why I don't want Jess to come, but something is tugging at me, telling me to just do this. *Sara, you are the one who needs to do this.*

"You're probably right. Maybe I will wait 'til we know what's going on. But this doesn't solve the home care issue. What about Parker, did you call him?"

Parker and his family are spending the month vacationing in Spain, specifically the Canary Islands.

"No, I haven't called him." My phone beeps. "It's work, gotta go." Call from Brett. *Shit.*

"Okay, I'll call Genevieve on her hospital room phone."

Neither Jess nor I even think about calling Raymond.

I switch gears and pray I don't get caught working at the hospital. I don't need any more pressure than I already have.

"Hi, Brett, sure, what do you need? Yes, I do have a draft ready to go for the Jordan marketing campaign. I can get that right over to you, just give me five minutes to get it into Dropbox. Bye." Why couldn't Brett have said, *Good job over the weekend, Sara.* How about, *I am so sorry I forgot to mention your contribution to the conference?* Or even, *How was your flight home?* I am so sick of this job.

I go back to my laptop, send off the report, and seriously wonder how long I can effectively pull off working under these circumstances. And I still need to try to figure out why I have found myself on Brett's you-are-not-my-favorite-person list.

Genevieve hangs up from talking with Jess just as I finish sending the report. "Can I get you anything? By the way, Genevieve, where's your cell phone?"

"Oh, that damn thing, I never remember to charge it. Why don't you go home? There is no need for you to stay here."

"I'm staying. I can help you figure out what the doctors are talking about and work at the same time. But it doesn't look like you'll be going home today."

"No, it doesn't. To be honest, I'm too weak to go home. What day is this, Sara?"

"It's Monday, Mom."

Genevieve dozes off and on for most of the afternoon and I try to focus on work. Finally, at six p.m., I call it a day, pack up, kiss my mother goodbye, and take the usual route down to my car.

On my drive home I call Jess. Again.

"Hi, I just left Genevieve and am heading home. I have nothing new to report other than what I told you earlier."

"She sounded really weak when I spoke with her this morning. I don't like this at all."

"She's really tired but doing okay. I think that she is extremely uncomfortable with the acid reflux or, as she likes to call it, Gerd."

"Okay, I will call her again to say goodnight. I hate that she doesn't use her cell. Talk tomorrow, bye." Jess hangs up.

I arrive home, exhausted—another long day, probably more so emotionally. Keith pours me a large glass of Chardonnay. He is a good man, I think as I gratefully accept the wine.

I just want to collapse on the couch with this wine, my husband, and our dogs, but that's not happening. Instead, I go into my home office, plug in my laptop, get out my notebook, and try to figure out more information on what ascites actually is, along with a bunch of other medical terms.

I sit back in my chair, sip my wine, and go over the

day's events. God, this is mind-boggling. Aside from the conversation with the doctor, Genevieve and I spent a good hour with the Patient Advocate, Mark Somebody. I need to get better with names. I wish everyone wore their name tags so I could read their stupid names. We talked about the different options and locations for rehabilitation centers. Genevieve decided on one closer to where Parker and I live.

"But Mom, wouldn't you rather be near your friends?" Do I really want her to stay in my town? I want this to end. I want Genevieve to just go home and be fine.

"No, it will be easier for you and your brother if I'm closer." Great, so we can be at your beck and call.

The next step was to see if Genevieve's choice, Grand Island Center, had a bed available. Mark called and it turned out they did, but of course, they needed to know when the patient was arriving. Since we don't know what is happening with Genevieve, Mark couldn't confirm a check-in date. Which meant the bed at GIC wasn't a sure thing. If she insisted on being close to us, then it had to be GIC, and I was adamant that this was where she should be. I didn't want her in some place where it felt like people were just left there to die. I have barely any experience visiting nursing homes or rehabilitation centers other than the one time I visited my father about fifteen years ago. He had simply disappeared from my life—the same was true for my sister and brothers. I started an online search for him and eventually found a Michael Austin, resident of the Goddard Center in Boston. I took a leap of faith, called the Center, identified myself, and they allowed me to visit. By that time, he was in the deep abyss of dementia. He had no idea who I was, so I never went back. Way too late to try to mend fences, bury the past, whatever you want to try to do to fix things. I do remember the Center was cold, not temperature-wise, just cold, stark, no warmth from the staff that I could see. I was actually grateful that he wasn't aware of his surroundings.

As I sit and discuss options for my mother, I can't imagine leaving her in a place like that. And, to add to all the cons of these types of places, she would hate the way they were decorated, or actually, the lack of taste is how she would put it. According to Genevieve, most people shouldn't be allowed to decorate. There aren't many options where we live so it really needs to be Grand Island Center. Fortunately, Mark agreed with us and said he'd do his best to make this work.

Mark then moved on to the insurance—what Genevieve's does and doesn't cover. "It's tricky," Mark explained, "you need to be careful when submitting the reason for care. If you say the patient is there just for monitoring then they cover only those expenses, not anything else, meaning no rehabilitation, no physical therapy. So, we need to be sure that you are admitted there for rehab, and then everything else such as the bed, meds, routine care, et cetera, is covered."

Genevieve's eyes had glazed over, and I was scribbling away in my notebook.

All this and we still don't know what the hell is going on. Is she ready to go to rehab or not? It's bad enough trying to understand what the doctors are saying, but this insurance stuff is a nightmare.

I want to scream, but instead, I finish my wine and go to bed.

DAY TWO

"The first lesson every child of Athena learned:
Mom was the best at everything, and you should never,
ever suggest otherwise."
– Rick Riordan

I'm up early this morning, showered, and out the door by seven-thirty. I remember what it was like working a nine-to-five office job. Something I absolutely do not miss. Now I can work in my pajamas all day if I want to. How-ever, I do try to not work in my pajamas all day because the last time I did, I went out to get the mail, forgetting what I had on, or that I hadn't combed my hair and wasn't actually sure if I had brushed my teeth. And, of course, that was when a silver Corvette slowed down, and the very handsome driver said, "Sara Austin, is that really you?" Oh shit. Steven. Oh shit, someone I hadn't seen in years. Steven and I had flirted with each other years ago, but it never went anywhere. I'm sure he was extremely grateful for that as he smiled at me with a rather quizzical look on his face. He was probably thinking, *She hasn't aged well.*

"Yup, it's me. Just getting the mail, and you caught me in my PJs," I said, smiling with my lips glued together, afraid I might have something in my teeth. "I work from home, and, well, sometimes I'm just so busy I don't have time to get dressed. You doing well? Nice to see you, gotta get back to work." Humiliated, I scurried back to the house, washed my face, brushed my teeth, and threw on a pair of jeans and a sweater.

Since then, I make the effort to change into yoga pants. I try to wash my face and brush my teeth before noon. Plus, you never know when Publisher's Clearing House could come knocking on your door with a camera crew ready to film you winning a million dollars.

Day two of coming to the hospital. Now I can maneuver the walk to my mother's room with no trouble. As usual, her floor is busy with the morning activities. Room 3799 is directly across from the nurses' station. I smile at the nurses and push open the door, ready for another day. Genevieve is asleep. I set up my 'office.' I seem to be getting into a rhythm with this situation.

"Is that you, Sara?"

"Yes, Mom, how did you sleep?"

"Why are you here? You don't need to be here; I can handle this."

"I told you, I'm staying 'til we figure this out. I don't know how you can handle it. I have a notebook to help me to know or even remember what they're talking about."

"Help me sit up, dear."

Genevieve is rail-thin. Is she eating anything, I wonder as I struggle to help all one hundred and nine pounds of her to sit up. "Put an extra blanket on my feet, I'm cold." Genevieve's ankles are terribly swollen, which looks so odd considering how stick-thin her legs are.

"Don't look at my ankles, it's awful. I have cankles. We

do not have cankles in this family," Genevieve says, as if anyone could do anything about cankles.

Yeah, just like we don't have cellulite in our family, Mommy dearest. Although Genevieve does not have cellulite, would never have cellulite, and this cankle thing is just temporary fluid retention.

"Are they letting you eat anything yet?"

"I tried to eat some broth last night."

"Were you able to keep it down?"

"I'm not vomiting, the food just comes back up and stays in my throat. It's a miserable feeling."

"Mom, how long has all of this been going on? You had said you haven't been feeling well since Christmas—has it been longer than that?"

"I'm not sure when it started, but the heartburn and food coming back into my mouth seemed to get significantly worse right after Christmas. But I didn't feel like myself before Christmas. Actually, I can't remember the last time I felt like myself," my mother says ruefully. "Sara, I didn't even decorate the house for the holidays."

"I thought Kathy helped you with that." Damn, when was the last time that I was at her house? Keith had picked her up last Christmas, but he wouldn't notice if the house was decorated or not. This is a huge wake-up call for me. Time to really step up, Sara—no more 'out of sight, out of mind' when it comes to Genevieve, at least for now. Looks like no outgoing tide in my immediate future.

"Kathy brought down the mantel decorations, but I was just too tired to instruct her where to place each piece."

"Why didn't you tell us?"

"What's to tell? Your old mother has heartburn and

doesn't feel like herself? What good would that do?"

"Mom, have you talked to Parker or Ray?" I ask, knowing that of course she hasn't.

"Not in a while," she says, evading the real question.

"Do they know you're in the hospital?"

"No."

"Why not? They should know."

"Parker is traveling, I don't want to worry him. I'll call Ray when I get home. I can and will let them know on my terms." Her words are firm, a tone that makes me cringe. That ended the conversation. *Maybe if you used your damn cell phone, you could call him now.*

I sit on the edge of my mother's bed, feeling exhausted, defeated. This isn't a new feeling for me, however, only Genevieve can make me feel quite like this. I learned at an incredibly young age when buttons should not be pushed. I am in no way in Genevieve Austin's league, meaning she would chew me up and spit me out without giving her words a second thought. Yeah, you would think I'd have a thicker skin, growing up as I did, but I don't. I am easily hurt. I am easily overlooked. I am convinced that I don't really matter. At least in the Austin family, and now, obviously, at work too.

I go back to my laptop and try to focus on work. Yes, I still need to work. We are a strange family, I think as I look over at my dozing mother.

Dr. Dalton comes in after lunch. "How are you today, Genevieve?"

Genevieve sighs. She is getting fed up with the same questions day after day. "I am the same as yesterday and the day before that. How many days have I been here?"

"Six days, Mom." Six days and nothing has changed.

Dalton looks uncomfortable. "Genevieve, we would like to do another CT scan this afternoon. Your first CT scan indicated ascites and we would like to assess for any possible progression versus any increased abdomen distension due to the small bowel obstruction."

Genevieve lets out another sigh. "Fine, if you think it will help you figure out what the hell is wrong with me."

I make a note: *Another CT.* None of this is making sense to me.

I return to my laptop and see I missed a message from Beth. *Call me tomorrow, at noon.*

Oh, simply great. The last thing I need is to have a call with one of the firm's partners. At this point, nothing is looking positive to me.

DAY THREE

"When we are no longer able to change a situation,
we are challenged to change ourselves."
– Viktor Frankl

I t's eight a.m., with the threat of snow in the forecast.

"Hi, Mom, how are you feeling today?"

"Oh, Sara, I told you not to come here every day."

"Well, good morning to you, too. Keith wants to visit. So does Liza," I say, putting my laptop on my desk and setting up for the day.

"Oh my god, absolutely not," Genevieve says in a tone that makes me cringe. It's a tone from my childhood, one that would cut me like a knife, taking the air right out of me.

"Why not? They want to see you," I say, pretending to still be setting up my workspace, fighting back the urge to just walk out of room 3799 and never come back.

"What, so Keith can just sit here looking at me? You know I adore him, but I don't want him coming. It's nice of him to offer, but that is not happening," Genevieve huffs.

"What about your granddaughter?"

"No. I do not want Liza to see me looking like this," she

says, running her fingers through her hair to try to fluff it a bit. I'm not surprised; my mother is extremely vain.

"Have you at least talked to Nicky since you were admitted? He should know." Nicky is Genevieve's lifelong friend. They have stood by each other since they were kids. He is a bit younger than Genevieve and I always felt he wished she could have been more than just a friend. Meme and Pops loved him like a son. A lifelong bachelor, Nicky lives in Florida and we consider him a part of our family.

"No, I haven't spoken with Nicky, nor do I plan to. I will once I'm home." Genevieve is getting agitated. "It's hell getting old, Sara. I am shocked that I'm still here, ninety-four years old. Never in my wildest dreams did I think that this would be happening."

"What did you think would happen?" I'm not sure where this conversation is going, not sure if I *want* to know where this conversation is going.

"I thought that I would have a stroke and die just like your grandmother did."

"I think that's called revisionist history. Meme had quite a few strokes, remember? She wound up in a nursing home and she was in a coma for days after the last one."

"Well, then, I just want to go to sleep and not wake up. The sooner the better," Genevieve says, smoothing her blanket over her distended lap. Her Siren Rose nails still look perfect.

Breathe, I think, breathe. "So, are you saying you want to die?"

"Yes. I want to die. I am so uncomfortable; I don't like pain and I am in pain. It's time, Sara. It is time for me to die." My mother says these words without a hint of uncertainty in her voice.

69

I feel a wave of sadness pass over me. Or is it compassion? I'm not sure. Why should I feel sad? My mother is ninety-four years old. She has had a pretty impressive life, but regardless, I am feeling something, and it's confusing me. I am not prepared to discuss dying with my mother, who is certainly going to die, probably sooner than I think I'm prepared for.

"I get it, and I see your point, no one wants to be in pain. Before we talk about dying, let's talk about you and your life. From where I stand, it looks like you've had a pretty amazing life. So, I guess the big question is, do you have any regrets?"

Without the least bit of hesitation, my mother says, "I regret ever meeting your father, that's what I regret. Biggest mistake of my life."

And she's back. Yup, that's the mother I know.

"Well, just think, if you hadn't met him, I wouldn't be sitting here with you right now," I snap at her, then get up and go back to the desk to work. This is what we do, I think. Genevieve throws out one of her barbs, I get hurt, and then I try to throw one back at her. But my barbs are never as sharp as hers.

I'm trying to focus on catching up on my emails, but I keep running the conversation with Genevieve through my head. I'm realizing that, at that moment, it was completely lost on both of us, mother and daughter, that we were having a very serious end-of-life conversation and we chose to act as if it never happened.

Knock, knock. "Hello." I turn in my chair to see May and Maureen tiptoe into the room.

"Come in, you two. Where have you been? I thought you would have been here sooner." Genevieve perks up, all smiles. So, she doesn't want to see her granddaughter or her son-in-law, but she has rallied for her neighbors? What the hell?

I get up to offer a kiss on the cheek to each of them. In their defense, May and Maureen, otherwise referred to as the "Ms," are much more to Genevieve than just neighbors. They are her best friends, her partners in crime. These three have a lot in common: love of theatre, great restaurants, beach sunsets—always enjoyed with a nice cocktail. They are good for each other. Genevieve bullied them into joining the gym with her, and when she could no longer drive, they were there for her, took her to doctors' appointments, food shopping, and so much more. Certainly, much more than we do for her, I think.

Damn. Jess is right. We need to find her help at home. We cannot expect these two to keep up the "errands" or Genevieve may lose her two best friends.

"What have you got there?" I ask, looking at the bags the Ms are holding.

"Oh, just a few things your mother asked us to bring to her," says May.

"Genevieve, I know you said you don't want to read but I brought you this anyway," Maureen says as she hands Genevieve the book *Being Michelle Obama.* "I loved this, and I think you will too."

May starts emptying out her bag, "This is the moisturizer you asked for, here is your night cream, and your serum and eye cream, hand cream, body moisturizer, reading glasses in case you change your mind about reading. Honestly, Genevieve, neither Maureen nor I will put up with you not reading. We need you to come home, drink with us, and discuss our latest favorite books."

"It takes a lot to look this good," Genevieve laughs, ignoring the reading comment.

"I'm going to go to the cafeteria and let you three visit," I say, grabbing my phone and purse.

I wonder why Genevieve doesn't want to read.

Down in the cafeteria, I get a coffee and sit alone at a table in the sun. The cafeteria has floor-to-ceiling windows that also look out to the harbor. It's a beautiful view, quintessential New England. Most of the big-money yachts are in dry dock or have been brought to warmer climates for the winter. Now you see the harbor for what it was originally intended, the Newport fishing fleet. The privately-owned fishing boats, the workhorses, are big and clunky; the once bright paint is fading on most of them. They may look worse for wear, but these boats are still doing their job, day in and day out. The sun feels soothing shining through the windows, and I am reminded of a poem I learned in elementary school, "The Fisherman" by Abbie Farwell Brown. I only remember a few of the lines, but it feels right at this very moment. *The fisherman goes out at dawn when everyone's abed, and from the bottom of the sea, draws up his daily bread. His life is strange; half on the shore and half upon the sea—Not quite a fish, and yet not quite the same as you and me.*

I need to find that poem again and reread it in its entirety, but back to reality. I sip my coffee and Google *What time is it in the Canary Islands?* After my conversation with Genevieve yesterday, I decided that, whether she likes it or not, I'm calling my brothers. There is no reason why Jess and I should be shouldering all of this.

"Hello," answers Parker.

"Hey, Parker, it's me, Sara."

"I know. I have caller ID. What's up?" It's ironic that I have been doing the same sarcastic dig to Jess, that Parker just did to me. Why are we such jerks to each other?

Parker sounds like I have interrupted him doing something that I'm sure is more fun, more interesting than what I've been doing lately.

"So, listen, the thing is, Genevieve is sick. She's been in Newport Hospital for six days now."

"Wow, that's a long time, what's going on?"

"A lot of things but nothing definitive. We seem to be in limbo right now. Oh, she doesn't want you or Ray to know."

"Why?"

"I have no idea," I answer, annoyed at his question. I am just freaking annoyed. I'm annoyed that I'm having this conversation, annoyed at my mother, annoyed at my brothers. I'm annoyed at the world at this moment.

"Do you think that we should come home?"

"No, I don't think so. You're there for what, another two weeks?"

"Yeah, we are. But we can change our plans if we need to. I'll call her. Does she have her cell?"

"No, don't call her yet. First, I need to tell her I told you. She's not going to be happy with me. I'll text you once I do. Of course, she doesn't have her cell. She's on the fourth floor, room 3799, under the name of Genevieve Austin," I finish sarcastically.

"Oh good, I wouldn't have known who to ask for when I call reception," he responds, equally sarcastic.

Next on the list, Ray.

"Well, hello, Sara."

"Hi, Ray, how are you doing?"

"I'm doing good, what's up? I can't remember the last time that we talked."

"Yeah, it's been a while. Listen, I need to tell you something." I repeat the same story I just told Parker. Ray's response is pretty much the same as his older brother's.

"No, don't call her yet. I'll text you later to let you know when it's a good time. Bye, Ray."

"Bye, Sara."

After I hang up, I sit quietly thinking about my youngest brother. What is going through his head right now? When was the last time I saw him? I know it's hard for Ray to feel any emotion, and it's not because he smokes a lot of pot or because he drinks more than he should. I think that it's because my brother generally feels emotionless. That's not to say Ray doesn't ever feel sad or happy, sure, he feels things, but Ray is more of a flatliner when it comes to emotions. Years ago, while in therapy, he told me that he was diagnosed with alexithymia, which is a condition where the person avoids emotionally close relationships. I am sure that if someone had asked Ray how he felt about his family he would just shrug his shoulders and probably say, "I don't know. I guess I don't feel much."

As far as his feelings for Genevieve go, Ray told me a few years ago that he finally came to understand that it was more of an obligation, rather than love, to acknowledge her. Like me, he had no great need to spend time with her, most likely because he felt that she never had a great need to spend time with him.

But, unlike me, Ray and Genevieve had a talk that I think drove the nail into the coffin. I'm not sure whose coffin, but it was pretty much the end for Ray and

Genevieve.

Ray had told me a number of years ago about a conversation that he had with Genevieve when he was a teenager. Genevieve told Ray in an unusual mother-son chat that she had wanted to get pregnant again after Parker for a very specific reason. "I thought maybe another boy, another son, would have made your father stop drinking, deal with reality, face up to his responsibilities. But you saw how that turned out," she had said.

So, after many years of therapy, Ray determined that he was a failed pawn in our parents' game of chess.

Okay, enough with this, it's time for me to call Beth. I go back up to the fourth floor, shut the door to the family room, which is thankfully empty again, and dial Beth's number. *Please let this room stay empty, please don't let a code red or something come over the intercom to give away where I am actually working.*

"Hi, Sara, how are you doing?" Beth says in her heavy South Jersey accent.

"I'm good. Hey, is this about the mix-up of slides for the Roman presentation?" Might as well just get this elephant out on the table.

"No, this isn't about that, but that was a major error and we still aren't sure if we won that account. We looked like amateurs, presenting ourselves as a premier marketing firm to a window treatment company and a fucking slide for the All is Well Beauty appears. I'm surprised that heads didn't roll because of that."

I didn't do it, I scream silently in my head. Once again I am voiceless. I am still intimidated to speak up, to actually defend myself, still afraid to hear harsh words spoken with disdain, words that might cut me like razors.

It's better to just be quiet, to protect myself.

"The reason that I want to talk with you is to let you know that Brett is moving some things around and you won't be reporting to him anymore. You're going to report directly to me. Unless of course you have an issue with that."

"No, of course not, no issue. I'm looking forward to it."

"Good. Since I have no idea what you do on a daily basis, put together a job description and get that over to me before the end of the day. We can meet later in the week to discuss."

"Okay, great. I'll get started on that now."

I hang up before Beth discovers that I'm not working from my home office. Shit, now I have to put together a stupid job description. Dammit, I don't have time for this bullshit. I am so sick of this stupid job. How many times am I going to say this to myself before I actually do something? Are things so bad between Brett and me that he feels he needs to dump me off on another partner of the company?

I get back to Genevieve's room just as the Ms are leaving.

May takes me aside. "Your mother told us that you have been her anchor, you're here every day, helping to sort out all of the medical jargon. I hope you know what a wonderful help you are to her. Maureen and I are just a phone call away. Whatever you need, Sara, we're here for you."

I am so uncomfortable with this type of conversation. I am not used to being praised or told that I am doing something right.

"Thanks, May. She might change her mind after I tell

her that I have called the boys."

"Oh dear, good luck. Come on, Maureen. We need to go." May pats my arm and the Ms are gone. I'm sure May knows that I've overstepped my boundaries and intruded onto Genevieve's turf.

"That was so nice of them to stop by," Genevieve says. "Sara, help me arrange my arsenal."

"Mom, I need to tell you something."

Genevieve stops fussing with the bottles and looks at me.

"I called the boys," I say defiantly, looking her right in the eye.

"Why would you do that? I told you not to call them. I specifically told you to not call them, Sara." Genevieve does not hide that she is annoyed with me. How dare I go against her wishes? So much for the "you are your mother's anchor" comment, not five minutes ago.

"I did it because it's not fair to them, it's not right that they have no idea what's going on here."

"Well, I certainly hope Parker isn't cutting his vacation short," Genevieve huffs.

"No, Mom, he isn't."

I catch a look of disappointment cross my mother's face.

DAY FOUR

"When we least expect it, life sets us a challenge to test
our courage and willingness to change; at such a moment,
there is no point in pretending that nothing has happened
or in saying that we are not yet ready. The challenge will
not wait. Life does not look back."
– Paulo Coelho

"Happy Valentine's Day, Genevieve."
It's eight a.m. at the hospital, which has now
become my routine, and another cold, grey February day
in Newport. I love living on the coast here in Rhode Island,
but the winters can be miserable. Not much snow, but a
lot of bone-chilling, damp days. What I wouldn't give to be
back in that warm Bahama sunshine, I think as I unpack
my supplies and set up for the day at my hospital desk.
Even though I've been home for just a few days, the
Bahamas seem like a distant memory. I turn away from
the window and begin my day.

I spent a good part of yesterday afternoon trying to put
together what I actually do for this company. I was never
given a job description when I was hired. My days are
never the same. How do I explain how I take a creative
concept, nurture it into an interactive design, and then

communicate that into a format for the art team and put in enough other crap to justify my salary? At this point I don't care, I did my best, and hope it's acceptable. I sent it to Beth just before five p.m.

"Hey, where did these beautiful flowers come from?" I ask.

"Aren't they lovely? They are from Jess. So thoughtful of her," Genevieve says.

"Yes, they are beautiful, and Jess is so thoughtful." I hope that didn't come out as insincere as I'm feeling. The flowers are beautiful, and it is a thoughtful gesture. But what about all of my gestures that have seemingly gone unnoticed? I feel like I am five years old. What about me? Look at what I've done, Mom.

"Good morning, Genevieve."

Oh, great, who's this? I think, forcing myself out of my wallowing.

"And who do we have here?" Genevieve asks.

"I'm Dr. Cook, and this is Dr. Tanner." Both doctors smile and nod their heads at the same time.

"More new doctors?" Genevieve asks, sounding annoyed.

"Yes, we're this morning's rounds team. We've received the results of your endoscopy and would like to discuss those findings with you and your daughter. You are Sara, correct?"

I nod and pull out my notebook.

"The biopsies that were taken showed a mild Schatzki ring in the lower third of your esophagus."

"What exactly does that mean?" Genevieve asks, sounding all businesslike.

Dr. Cook goes on to explain, "A Schatzki ring is a

narrowing of the lower esophagus that can cause dysphagia. It's comprised of a small tissue fold that partially blocks the esophagus, leading to dysphagia. Dysphagia simply means difficulty in swallowing. The dysphagia itself is rather common and occurs in about three percent of the population."

"So how do you cure this?" she asks.

I'm scribbling away, letting my mother take the lead on this.

"There isn't a cure for Schatzki rings," explains Dr. Tanner. "However, there are treatments for this condition that will allow solid food to pass more freely. But we can discuss that at a later date. Also, your second CT scan showed no change to the ascites, but there are signs of ileus. We need to determine if this is due to the bowel obstruction."

"Wait a minute," I interrupt, "what does any of these have to do with the other findings, the bowel obstruction, the ascites, and now this thing ileus?" I look over at Genevieve. She looks concerned.

"What did you say, ileus? What in god's name does that mean? Why can't you people speak plain English?" Yes, Genevieve is concerned and getting pissed off. Not a good combination.

Dr. Cook steps a bit closer to Genevieve's hospital bed and calmly answers her question. "The detection of ileus could indicate an abdominal infection, which causes partial or complete blockage of either the large or small intestine."

"We would like to perform a paracentesis to determine what the three major concerns are, to answer your question, Sara," interjects Dr. Tanner. "And we would like to schedule it for this afternoon."

"No, I am done, I don't want anything else done to me."

We all turn and look at Genevieve. She is looking right back at us with fierce determination. She has said no. This is her final answer.

"Okay, hold on, what is this paracentesis procedure like?" I ask the doctors while looking at my mother. "It might be nothing, Mom."

Dr. Cook's turn. "Paracentesis is a minimally invasive procedure. A small tube is inserted into the side of your abdomen to drain the fluid. Then the fluid is sent to pathology, which should help us narrow down the root cause of your symptoms."

"Absolutely not," Genevieve responds.

"Mom, I will do whatever you want, the decision is yours and I will stand by you, back you up, this is your life. But this procedure might help them—us—to figure out what is going on with you. You've been in the hospital for eight days now and we still don't have a diagnosis.

"You"—I turn away from my mother and look at the two doctors, letting them see a pissed-off Sara Austin—"have given us nothing but confusing, conflicting explanations as to why Genevieve is sick. Very simply, is this procedure safe? Can this procedure be done with anesthesia; so, pain-free, and will this procedure actually give us answers?" Wow, where the fuck did that come from. I stood up, I spoke firmly, I stayed in control, there wasn't a tear, a shaky voice, or a hint of uncertainty in my demeanor. I need to bottle this energy and keep it in my purse for whatever might happen at any given moment.

"This procedure is quite safe, and it does not warrant anesthesia. It is, as I said, minimally invasive."

Oh, that is not the right answer, Doctor What's-your-name, I say to myself. I'm starting to fume. *Keep it together Sara.*

"Then I'm not doing it."

I am beginning to think that Genevieve and I make a pretty good team.

"Genevieve, this is the only way we can determine the cause of your symptoms. If nothing else, once the fluid is drained you will feel much better. Your stomach will be less distended, which will relieve a lot of the pressure you're feeling."

"I am a chicken. I hate pain. Anesthesia. Or I am not doing it." Genevieve is determined and it is quite evident that nobody is pushing her into anything she doesn't want to do. But Genevieve is certainly not a chicken—what a strange thing for her to say. Is she scared? She's never scared, I think as I look at my mother staring down two doctors.

"If that's the only way you'll agree to do this, then I'll see what I can for you. Let me check with the anesthesiologist team. We are going to have to jump through hoops for them to agree. This will delay the procedure, so it won't be this afternoon."

"Then I suggest you start jumping right now." Genevieve has gotten her point across to these two doctors.

The doctors leave, probably wondering how the hell they were going to pull this off.

"Sara, what day is this?"

"It's Thursday, Mom."

"Go home, dear. I am tired, so I'm going to rest for the afternoon. I think you and I have given those doctors some work to do."

I took advantage of this reprieve to make some calls on the drive home, hoping nobody from work needed anything.

First is Liza, to update her on her grandmother's situation. I'm trying to sound upbeat. "Looks like a nursing home for a week or so and then Genevieve should be able to come home."

"I really want to come to see her. Has she changed her mind about seeing me?"

My heart breaks for my daughter. Liza is such a beautiful, gentle, sensitive soul. Being told your grandmother doesn't want to see you doesn't do much for your sense of self. Unfortunately, or maybe fortunately, I do know how my daughter feels. I just hope that I have shown her how much she means to me; how important it is to have her in my life. Genevieve Austin is not the mother of the year. It's sometimes hard to mother when you don't have a good example. When you don't really have a mother.

"Oh, you know how she is, she won't see Keith either. She actually told me not to tell your uncles."

"You told them, right?" Liza asks.

"Of course." We both laugh just a little bit.

Liza and I hang up. I dread the next call on my list.

"Hello?"

"Hi, Emma, it's Sara."

Emma is Genevieve's ninety-two-year-old sister, my aunt. They are complete opposites; Emma is a conservative, religious devotee. Genevieve is a liberal and has no time for religious restrictions, but they are great friends, choosing to let their differences go. In other words, they don't talk about them. This arrangement has been working pretty well for years—ninety years, in fact.

"Well, Sara, this is a surprise. Everything okay?"

"Everything is good, except that Genevieve is in the hospital."

"Oh, dear, what happened? I haven't talked to your mother in a while."

"She's been there for a few days"—lie number one—"and they are working on determining what is going on."

"Well, what happened?"

I fill my aunt in as much as I feel Emma needs to know. It wasn't that I was trying to hide anything, but I can tell that I am changing. I think that I'm starting to feel protective of Genevieve, I am starting to feel in charge. Maybe it started when I spoke up to Dr. Cook, more so today with the doctors, but regardless, something was shifting in me.

"I have some time before this evening's Mass, I'll go over to say hi."

"That might not be a good idea, Emma. Genevieve is having a procedure done tomorrow and they want her to rest. She is exhausted." Lie number two. I hope this will keep Emma from driving over to the hospital.

"Oh, that doesn't bother me, I'll just pop in."

You are not an easy lady to dissuade, I think, assuring Emma that I will call her tomorrow.

The last call is to Jess.

"Hello?"

"Hey, do you have a minute? I'm driving home and thought I could fill you in on today's events."

"I have more than a minute," Jess says. "I talked to Genevieve a while ago, she said something about another procedure. But she sounded confused about what it is, only that they are going to drain the fluid out of her abdomen. That sounds awful. What's going on? I tried calling you, but you didn't pick up."

"I have been on the phone with Emma, shoot me now." I explain to my sister the latest findings, butchering the medical terms bounced around the hospital room this morning.

"This has gone on for too long. I think we should get her into a Boston hospital. Seriously, Boston has some of the finest hospitals in the country. It might be time to get her out of Hicksville."

"I think that the best course of action at this point is to do the procedure as soon as they can arrange for the anesthesiologist, get the results, and take it from there." I come across as very matter of fact—this is what we are doing, damn it. The shift in me is growing.

"Just one other thing. Genevieve doesn't want to read. I find this to be so strange, she loves to read. I also noticed that she barely has her television on. That I can understand, but I don't understand the not reading thing."

"Oh no, I don't like to hear that."

"Why, do you know something I don't?"

"No, but remember that Meme stopped reading altogether when she got really sick? Don't you remember? She just stopped and then a few weeks later she died. Oh dear, I don't like this at all."

I decide not to tell my sister about the conversation between Genevieve and me yesterday. I decide not to tell my sister that our mother really wants to die. I know in my heart that this time is different from when she was first admitted to the hospital. This is real. Genevieve means business this time.

DAY FIVE

"To be tested is good. The challenged life
may be the best therapist."
– Gail Sheehy

It's Friday, finally—the end of a challenging week.

I arrive at the hospital earlier than usual. This morning I got a voicemail from one of the nurses on the fourth floor, letting me know that Genevieve's procedure would be sometime this morning. I'm anxious about it. I don't want to miss anything, any conversations or visits from any doctor, nurse, or anyone who has anything to do with my mother's care.

Genevieve is asleep; she looks vulnerable. I never thought I would use those words to describe my mother. I set up my laptop, same as the last five days. Fortunately, it has been a fairly quiet work week, other than the Beth/Brett situation. Maybe the marketing team is still recovering from the amazing two-day convention I put on for them. Oh wait, that wasn't me, that was Lexi Hanson. I really need to get back to meditating and stop being so negative. Quiet work week or not, I have back-to-back conference calls scheduled for this afternoon. God, I hope that nobody wants to use the family room, which I have started to claim as my own.

"Oh, is that you Sara? I told you not to come today. I'm having that damn procedure sometime this morning." The queen has woken.

"And good morning to you, Mother," I say sarcastically, but with a softness to the jab. "How was your night?"

"I was restless. I have a lot on my mind."

Tread carefully here, I think. "I am sure you do, but what kept you up last night?"

"I was thinking about death, about dying."

I swallow hard, try to get rid of the lump that just formed, try to not let my mother see that I can't breathe. I remove my emotions, a process which I excel at, and say, "What do you think about death?"

"Well, I think it is quite final."

"Do you believe in the afterlife?"

"I have heard of that, but I'm not quite sure what that even means."

I find that odd. Genevieve is so well-read. I'm surprised that she hasn't dipped a toe into the divine, spiritual, or mystical books. How could she not have read *The Celestine Prophecy, A Course in Miracles, The Art of Happiness,* or *A New Earth*? I have them all, although that doesn't mean I've read them all front to back—maybe I should.

Our family is not what you would call a religious family. Genevieve was brought up Catholic—her mother, Margaux, converted from Protestant to Catholicism so she could marry our grandfather. They went through the motions, attended church on Sundays, celebrated Christmas and Easter, gave up something for Lent, went to confession on Fridays, and always offered up a few dollars for the collection.

Genevieve and Michael raised us the same way, but a step up. For the few years that Dad was sober, while we were young, our parents were prominent members of St. Peter's, the local church. Michael collected offerings during the Sunday services, they entertained the parish priests for dinner, we attended Sunday school. Jess and Parker embraced their religion and thrived in Sunday school. Both went on to go to parochial school.

I questioned everything about Catholicism. I started at a young age, asking questions about things that made no sense to me, and I think this embarrassed my parents. Seriously, how could the Father, the Son, and the Holy Ghost be one person? I despised Sunday school, and for Lent, I would give up hot fudge sundaes which were rarely offered anyway in the Austin house. Ray was too young then to go to church or Sunday school. After the tsunami, Genevieve brought us to church less and less. She arranged for riding lessons for me on Sunday mornings and left Ray with Meme. Jess and Parker would go to church with friends. After I received my confirmation in the eighth grade, Genevieve asked me if I wanted to continue going to church. "Hell no" was my response and that was the end of religion as we knew it in the Austin family. Jess and Parker still try to get to church every Sunday. I have serious doubts about Ray going to church— any church.

"Well, I'm sure you have heard stories of near-death experiences, or souls letting their loved ones know that they're all right. People having premonitions and acting on them. You know, when your gut, your intuition kicks in. You've had those things happen to you, right?"

"No, I haven't."

"Mom, you know that Meme and Aunt Madeline were intuitive, right?"

"Sara, your grandmother did not share a lot with me, so if you say she was, then so be it."

I'm dumbfounded by her response. Genevieve grew up surrounded by women who were inherently aware of things beyond what was in plain sight. Her mother, her grandmothers on both sides, and Aunt Madeline, who was only a few years older than Genevieve, treasured and re-spected their intuitive abilities. As a child, I absorbed their stories like a sponge. It isn't anything you learn in a book. Meme showed me how to acknowledge what was deep in my psyche, to accept what is a gift, our ability to open ourselves to the universe. But only when the time was right and only when we were ready. She taught me to look for signs and to accept that I was seeing signs for a reason. For example, a red cardinal is a spiritual message from a lost loved one to let you know they're still with you.

When I was a teenager, I had a strict eleven p.m. curfew on Friday nights, the only night I was allowed out. I always made sure I was home on time. On a few occasions, after I was in bed when I was supposed to be, I would hear a phone ring at the same time, every time, eleven-thirty. It was always just one ring, so clear that, at first, I'd start to get out of bed to answer it. I finally told Meme what I had been experiencing, telling her that it seemed odd that nobody else heard it, and that it was always just one ring.

"Sara, I believe that is your father thinking of you, hoping that you are home, safe in bed, by eleven-thirty." I never questioned this, never told Genevieve, but it did make me feel good, maybe a little bit special. Maybe I did still have that knight in shining armor nearby.

I know that I'm not getting through to Genevieve.

"All right, how about this? There is a story about a little kid, maybe three years old, who went up to his new baby sister or brother and his parents overhear him say, 'Tell me about God, I am forgetting him.' Mom, this is profound stuff. There is more to death than we know."

"Well, since I haven't personally experienced any of that, I am not sure I believe anything you just said."

Even now, with this important conversation, Genevieve can still be difficult. Her views are the only views of any value.

"What do you believe? Do you believe in anything?" I ask after releasing a big sigh. Fortunately, she didn't hear it.

"I believe that when you die, you return to the earth. You quite simply return to earth and become dirt. Sara, I am going to die, we are all going to die, let's change the subject and discuss what I would like to happen after I am gone."

"Okay." I shrug my shoulders, another possible breakthrough moment cut off at the knees. I get my notebook out of my laptop bag and begin writing down my mother's final wishes, which are surprisingly low-key. Genevieve provides the names of people she wanted to be called. "Have Parker do that; I don't want him to feel left out. I want a small graveside service, family only. Please make sure they know to dress to impress, and don't forget the AstroTurf."

I sigh again; this is all so exhausting. "Genevieve, you said that the Cemetery Board vetoed any AstroTurf on the grounds."

"Oh, the hell with them. You'll need to give them a call, the cemetery people, not the board people. The headstone is ready to go, it just needs an end date. There is a nice man who works there, tell him you're my daughter, he'll help you out. After the service, I'd like a tasteful luncheon at the house, invite the names I just gave you. Sara, you decide on the food, something sophisticated, oh, and only white wine, no liquor. I don't want anyone getting drunk at this. I want people to speak about me, as long as it's complimentary."

Ha, the only ones getting drunk at this will be your kids, I think, just as a nurse's assistant comes in the room with a wheelchair.

"Genevieve, we're ready to take you down for the paracentesis."

"Is there an anesthesiologist waiting?"

"Yes, ma'am, there certainly is. We don't know how Dr. Cook did it, but he said you wanted to be sedated and he made sure that this is what is gonna be done. You must be something special, Genevieve Austin, because I have never seen this procedure done with any type of sedation."

Genevieve has a smug little smile. "Sara, no need to wait for me," she says as she's wheeled out of her room.

I sit alone in my mother's room. I've never been alone in this room; Genevieve has always been here. The emptiness is overwhelming; the silence, even with all the noise on the floor, is deafening. Things are starting to make sense to me, the shift becoming more pronounced. My mother is preparing to die, she knew it at Christmas, and now I know in my heart that Genevieve knew that would be her last Christmas. I will do everything in my power to do what my mother wants; I won't let anyone stand in my way or stop me. I need to make one more call before I dial in for the marketing conference call.

"Hello, Longview Cemetery."

"Yes, hello, this is Sara Austin and, ummm, well, my grandparents have a plot there, is that what you call it, a plot? And anyway, my mother, well, she isn't...um, passed, I mean she hasn't passed yet. I guess I have questions, but I don't know what they are." I'm stumbling over my words; I have no idea how to start this conversation. *Yeah, hi, my mother might die soon, do I need to make a reservation ahead of time to bury her?*

"Well, hello, Sara, my name is Nate Eldridge. I am the cemetery manager. Since I have some experience in this line of work," he says, clearing his throat, "I think we should start from the beginning, okay?"

"Okay." I feel only a bit relieved.

"Now, you said your grandparents have a plot with us. What's their last name?"

"Lemaire."

"Let me see here, would that be Edward Lemaire?"

"Yes."

"That's a lovely piece of property, corner lot overlooking the eighteenth hole of the golf course. Hold on, are you related to the two sisters that come here about twice a year to visit their parents' plot?"

I am squirming in my chair. "Yes, I believe I am related to those two."

"Oh my goodness, we love those two characters, funny as all get-out. I remember one—what's her name?—the one that wanted to have AstroTurf put in."

"Yes, that would be Genevieve."

"Right, Genevieve and Emma. They would come here,

like I said a couple of times a year, just come in and sit in the office and talk about the condition of the plot. Oh, are you calling about one of them?"

"Yes, I'm calling about my mother, Genevieve."

"Oh, I am sorry." Nate turns serious.

"Well, the thing is, I mean, what I am trying to say is..." I am tripping over my words—how am I even having this conversation? "Genevieve is still with us, but, I guess, the question is for how long? She's told me what she wants as far as her service goes, so I guess I need some help on how to do this, please."

"Of course. I'm here to help, that's what I do. Let me ask you some questions and we can go from there. To start off, your mother was proactive, her headstone is already engraved. So, you're in good shape there."

I am wondering if I can get a nurse to bring me an IV of vodka. How can I be in good shape just because my mother has had her own headstone done?

"You said your mother told you what she wants to take place at the graveside, is that correct?"

"Yes, something simple, just the immediate family. I don't know what day or time yet, but I do know that she wants AstroTurf."

Nate laughs just a tiny bit. "Let's discuss the AstroTurf in a minute. Sara, will there be a church service?"

"No."

"Do you want or need an officiant at the family graveside service?"

"No."

"Okay, sounds quite simple, and we are here to make sure that this goes according to you and your mother's plans."

Shit, I want to cry, now I want to cry. Nate, don't be so nice to me, please, I need to stay resolute, focused. I need to be the strong one.

"Sara, all you need to do at this point is call us when the time comes, and we will complete the engraving and work with you on the graveside arrangements. At that time, you will need to file the death certificate and supply us with a copy."

"How much advance notice do you need? I can't give you a date." How can I give you a freaking date, she is still alive, I scream inside my head. I think I have amped up the screaming in my head lately.

"I don't need any notice. You just focus on your mother for now."

I actually take a huge breath. Thank you, Nate Eldridge, for helping me to breathe.

"Thank you so much, Nate, you have taken a deer in the headlights and done, well, I don't know what you've done, but I can see a bit clearer now. So, can we talk AstroTurf?"

The Lemaires do have a family plot overlooking Ed Lemaire's favorite Newport golf course. He and Margaux are buried there, with the epitaph *"Par pour le court."* The plot is large enough for six family members. However, Genevieve chose her own epitaph and took over the back of the large headstone with the inscription "Genevieve Anouk Lemaire, beloved daughter, cherished Mother, July 12, 1924 to..." All that is missing is what comes after the word "to." Genevieve left no room for any other family members to have their names and dates included.

This proved a problem when Genevieve's younger brother died before her. He ended up with a simple marker with just his name, date of birth, and date of death. And on Veteran's Day a flag.

The plot isn't kept up. Not that it has dying balloons and moldy angel statues, it just doesn't have any grass or plantings. That would mean watering, watering means maintenance, maintenance means somebody needs to go there, and that means somebody needs to care. The only people that seemed to care about the upkeep of the Lemaire plot are ninety-two and ninety-four years of age. Genevieve was beside herself with how "shabby" it all looked. And that is when she decided the answer to it all was AstroTurf. The true designer that Genevieve is, her outings with Kathy turned to scouting out different AstroTurf locations so she could compare and judge the quality. According to Genevieve, the best example of the most natural-looking AstroTurf was right in your own backyard, which is how she presented her request to the Cemetery Board. "I have done quite a bit of research on AstroTurf and the most natural model is at the high school right here in your town."

"Oh, your mom and her sister, what a couple of hoots. We loved having them come visit. Sometimes we would all pile in the car and drive to the plot. They would go on and on about how shabby it looked compared to the neighbors. I would always tell the sisters the same thing, the neighbors are a large local family with nothing to do but take care of their plot. That didn't quiet your mother down. I think that she thought she could work around the Board. Oh, I am so sorry to hear she is ill."

In the end, Genevieve was told that Longview is a cemetery, not a football field.

Nate and I hang up. I feel a bit better. I am an

organizer; I like to know what to expect. I check this off my list. This was a big one, I think, dialing into the work conference call, still wishing I could get an IV of vodka. "Yes, hello everyone, Sara here."

I hate them all right now.

It's five p.m.—I'm home earlier than usual. Genevieve was wiped out after the procedure, so I logged off from work and left the hospital.

Keith and I have settled into an unsettling routine. I leave earlier than him in the morning and arrive home later than him in the evening. He usually has leftovers warming and I fill him in on the latest Genevieve updates.

"Hi, I'm home," I yell as my dogs come charging for attention. Keith is on the phone, kisses my cheek, and returns to the call. "I will make myself a big fat vodka, just vodka, nothing else," I say loudly. He looks at me, still on the call, and shakes his head no. "Yup, I'm quite capable of doing that," I say, slowly walking to the liquor cabinet. "Genevieve would be appalled if she knew I was making my own cocktail, but I can do it."

Keith ends his call. "No way, Sara, I don't need Genevieve coming after me, I'm making your drink, go sit."

One bit of advice that I took from Genevieve is, "Darling, never make your own cocktail if you can help it." I smile, taking my drink from Keith, and silently thank my mother and giving Keith a kiss.

I fill Keith in on Genevieve, the disquieting discussion we had about death and the afterlife, what happened at work, and Nate at the cemetery. Then I bring my cocktail to the bathroom, and sink into a tub of steaming hot water, let out a big sigh, and think back a few days, to Lorna, the nursing assistant. I wonder where she got her confidence, her self-esteem, her great sense of self? In my world, someone who weighs whatever she weighs, maybe two hundred pounds, would be dismissed, considered broken, not worth our time, they must be weak, stay away. But I witnessed a beautiful woman prepared to take Genevieve's barbs and deflect them with dignity and grace. Lorna is probably praying for that skinny white woman with good nails. I need to be more like Lorna. I need to find that sense of self, embrace it, and truly own it. I take another sip and let the day wash away.

DAY SIX

"Into the ocean I go, I slip into your arms, I let you hold
me, envelop me in your waves, you let me breathe, as I
dive deep into your world, my world, our world,
I breathe, I float, I am."

– J. L.

It's Saturday. I sleep in just a bit and relish in the
slowness of my morning, coffee in bed, dogs curled up
next to me. For a split second I feel normal. But reality can
be a harsh awakening.

"Keith, I'm going to shower and head over to the hospital today. I'll call Genevieve first to see if she needs
anything. I hope it's a quick in-and-out visit." My phone
rings.

"Hi, Jess."

"Hi, Sara, I just talked with Genevieve, she sounds so
much better this morning."

"Seriously, Jess, it's like six a.m. for you, you're crazy."

"I'm just worried; it's so hard being this far away. But
I will say that I do feel a bit relieved that she sounds like
she's getting stronger."

"Let's hope so. Maybe yesterday's procedure is her
ticket out of the hospital into rehab for a few days, and

98

things get back to normal."

"Sara, things are never going to get back to normal. First of all, what exactly is normal when it comes to Genevieve? We are still going to need to figure out what to do for her, care-wise. I don't think she should go home. She's starting to forget things. I am afraid she is going to burn the house down."

Okay, now I just want to go back to bed and pull the covers over my head. Instead, I tell my sister I'll call her later, shower, have a second cup of coffee, and call Genevieve.

"Hello?"

"Hi, Mom, it's me, Sara."

"Oh, hello dear." I can hear voices in the background.

"Are you busy?"

"Well, I have a room full. May and Maureen just got here, and Emma came in earlier, and Kathy called, she's coming to visit this afternoon."

"You sound good, better."

"I am so much better. Sara, I am good today, stay home, please."

A rare occurrence—I do what my mother says. Keith and I walk the dogs on the beach, breathing in the cold, clear air. Funny that I can always breathe at the beach, I think, feeling both sad and grateful at the same time. Our dogs love running free on the flats, chasing the seagulls. This is pure joy for them, for me, too. The beach has always been my place in good times and in bad times. The ocean is in my blood—actually, it's in most Austins' blood. We have been coming to the beach since we were babies. Genevieve would put each baby out in the sun as soon as it warmed up, regardless of our age, two months, six months, it didn't matter to her. "I used to rotate you all like little pigs to get you started on your summer tan." We spent all of our childhood summers living with Meme and Pops at their summer house on Gooseberry Beach. Genevieve would drop us off in June, on the last day of school, and bring us home on Labor Day. It was a wonderful, big, comfortable house—nine bedrooms, a wraparound porch, walking distance to the local shops and the library. I have such sweet memories of walking to the library with Meme, stopping at the bakery on the way home for croissants. The ocean was our front yard, and the side yard was large enough to "shoot some balls," which we would do after dinner. Each child had their own driver and putter, and if it wasn't golf outside, then it was gin rummy inside. Jess, Parker, and I would sit around the big kitchen table with our grandparents playing for pennies. Summers were carefree. Our grandparents were extremely laid back when it came to watching over us. When we were young, we had a local college student in charge who would return each summer to babysit us. Why not? The pay was good, and she could work on her tan while Ray stayed in his playpen and the rest of us played in the waves, went out over our heads, and stayed in the ocean until we were purple. In other words, the Austin kids' summer days were pretty much without supervision, and in my mind summers were idyllic.

As I walk along the shoreline, I think, funny that my happy memories don't include my parents. Actually, that's not funny. But as I bend down to inspect a piece of sea glass, I have a flash of my twenty-two-year-old self, two-year-old baby Liza, and a dog in tow, moving back to Newport on my own. I was forming my own family as a single mother; this was an awfully hard time in my life.

I am a child of the sixties. Sounds like something out of AA. Hi, my name is Sara, and I am a child of the sixties.

I more than embraced free thinking, free love, freedom from my family. I ate, slept, and breathed freedom. When I was about thirteen years old, I came into my own, or more importantly went out on my own. I looked good on paper, pretended to do all the right things that were expected of me, but inside I was empty. I was too young then to realize that I had lost so much in the tsunami and now it was catching up with me. My friends became my family, and I drifted away from the Austins little by little until they were lost to me. I skipped school, marched against the Vietnam war, wore bell-bottoms, Frye boots, smoked pot, and looked every bit the part of a sixties teenager. Home, yes, I still lived at home then and that was a challenge for me, for Genevieve, and probably for Parker and Ray. Jess had moved out by then. I didn't realize how lucky I was to have a nice home, good meals, a car to use when my mother allowed. None of this registered or mattered to me. I was, at that point in my life, trying to come up for air from the tsunami. Or considering letting the air go, letting myself go, down deep into the ocean that I loved. It was an exceedingly difficult time for me. I guess I would call it typical teenage angst on steroids, rebellious with no parental support or love. Genevieve and I were always at odds. The more rules she put in place to keep me in line, the more defiant I became. My breaking point with my mother happened the day I came home from school and went into my bedroom and thought that we had been robbed. Drawers were pulled out, clothes were thrown all over the place, my mattress was on the floor. Terrified, I called my mother at work. That's when she told me she had read my diary. We hadn't been robbed. It was my mother who had an absolute psychotic reaction to the words I wrote and tore my room apart in a fit of rage.

"How could you read my diary?" I asked. "That's private."

"You left it out for me to read," was her motherly response. "After reading what you wrote about me, how much you hate me and hate your life, what did you expect I would do, Sara? You wish you were never born? Some days *I* wish you were never born."

Fuck you! I did not leave it out for you to read, is what I wanted to say. Instead, I slammed down the phone and took half a bottle of aspirin. I'm not sure what was going through my undeveloped thirteen-year-old brain, I just knew I needed to make the pain go away.

What is strange about this story is that Dad, who was never around, stopped by out of the blue. I don't know why I told him what I had done but I did. He acted like a parent and called our family doctor, who said just keep an eye on me. When Genevieve came home, Dad told her what I had done. My charming mother's response was, "I wish she had taken the whole bottle. Where is she? I can find plenty more pills for her to take."

"Genevieve, stop. You don't mean that, don't say that. What if Sara can hear you?" My father was pleading with her.

"I most certainly do mean it. I hope she can hear me. Sara, I hope you heard that I have plenty of pills if that's what you want," she yelled. "And what the hell are you doing here, Michael? You can't just show up when you feel like it. Those days are long gone, Michael Austin. Divorced, remember? We are divorced." Genevieve was boiling with anger.

"Genevieve, please stop."

She cut him off mid-sentence. "Get out, Michael, go back to wherever it is you live. Do you even have a place to live, or are you sleeping in your car? God, both you and Sara make me sick. Get out."

I was sitting at the top of the stairs listening to my mother's reaction to her daughter's pain, my pain, and she just stuck a fucking harpoon into my heart. I was thunderstruck by what I had just witnessed. I stood up from the stairs, walked into my room, and shut the door. Out of my bedroom window, I watched my father back his car out of the driveway. My five-minute knight in shining armor was struck down by the evil queen and he left me with her. This was the moment that I stopped being able to take a deep breath.

From that moment on, I went through the motions of life. Genevieve and I never discussed what transpired that afternoon, and neither did my father and I. That's what we do in this family. We look away, ignore, deny any feelings. We don't share or discuss anything. We are like the Stepford wives, or rather, the Stepford family. That is every one of us but Genevieve.

I finished high school with no intention of going to college. Actually, there was no encouragement from anyone for me to think about college. Not my family, not a teacher, not my guidance counselor.

I was drifting. If I had been in counseling I might have been diagnosed with alexithymia, the same as Ray. Probably all of the Austin kids suffer from that.

After high-school graduation, I met Tom. We had gone

to school together, but I had never even noticed him. I met him because he was selling some pot and I was looking to buy it. We dated, I got pregnant, and we married quietly one month before Liza was born. No one from my family was invited. I never had any feelings for him, and I divorced him a year later. I didn't have feelings for anyone other than my new baby.

Yet today, with all that baggage behind me, I am remembering my mother's support of my decision to walk away from a dysfunctional marriage and start over, with pretty much nothing but my baby and my dog. Genevieve didn't provide financial support, and it wasn't as if she was there helping with Liza, but somehow, I knew she had my back. I didn't feel that too often. As I started over as a single mother, it was my mother who stood up for me. She pressured Pops to buy me a car so that I could be somewhat independent. Genevieve told me that the key to life is independence.

The squawking seagulls brought me back to the present. I tossed the piece of glass—not quite perfect enough to be a part of my large sea glass collection—back into the ocean. In life, I chose independence over what others perceive as perfection.

I continued to drift, but now I had the responsibility of a child. Liza went to daycare and I worked, eventually finding a job I loved, working with young families at risk. I had finally found something that gave me energy, something to look forward to, something that made me feel valuable.

My cell phone rings, breaking up my moment of reflection. "Hello?"

"Hello, is this Sara Austin?"

I am always hesitant when a phone call starts out like this. "Who's calling?" I ask shortly.

"This is Dr. Cook. I met you and your mother on Wednesday. I wanted to let you know that your mother did quite well with the sedation and the paracentesis procedure, which took just under sixty minutes. We removed thirty-three hundred milliliters of fluid, which was sent to cytology, and we are waiting for those results. The morning team let me know that Genevieve is feeling much improved. I am sure that removing that fluid has lessened her pain, which appears to be a relief to her."

"That is great news, just the fact that she is feeling better is great news. So, what are the next steps?" I am blown away by the fact one of Genevieve's many drive-by hospital doctors has taken the time to call me on a Saturday.

"We wait for the results, which should be in the next couple of days."

"Thank you, I so appreciate the call."

Life is good, I say to myself.

DAY SEVEN

"I'm not afraid of death; I just don't want
to be there when it happens."
– Woody Allen

I wake up early, too early for a Sunday. Keith and I are cozy under our comforter, drinking coffee in bed, talking about Genevieve, the prognosis—or, rather, lack of prognosis—and the uncertainty of the future.

"It's so frustrating," Keith says, sipping his coffee. "But, Sara, I think you need to prepare for what may lie ahead. Your mother is ninety-four years old. I know that she doesn't act it or look it, but I wonder how much her body can withstand. She hates the treatments, hates the hospital, hates not feeling good. Does she need to sell the house and move to a retirement center that has nursing care? Because you know that she'll refuse to do that. From everything you've told me it doesn't sound like she can go home unless there is round-the-clock nursing care there. Seriously, what is the solution here?"

"I know, this being in limbo sucks. I can't even imagine what it must be like for her. I'm going to shower and go visit for a little bit. I wish you could come. Thanks for the coffee." I give Keith a quick kiss on the cheek, jump out of bed, and practically run to the bathroom, hands over ears. Shut up, shut up, shut up. I cannot deal with one more fucking thing. And now it appears that my husband is facing my reality for me.

"Yup, this does suck," I hear Keith say.

My cell phone rings just as I'm about to pull out of my driveway. Emma. I sigh.

"Hello?"

"Hello, Sara, this is Emma." Obviously, Emma isn't aware of a little thing known as caller ID.

"Hi, Emma, how are you this morning? Shouldn't you be at church?"

"I'm going to the eleven o'clock Mass today. I thought I'd mix things up a bit," my aunt says with a chuckle. "Sara, do you have a few minutes? I want to talk to you about Genevieve. You know I saw her yesterday?"

"Is she okay? Is there something I should know about?" I'm on high alert. What happened between yesterday and this morning?

"Oh, your mother is fine, dear. Well, as fine as anyone can be at her age. We had a lovely visit yesterday morning reminiscing about our lives, our victories, and our defeats. I got to the hospital fairly early. Genevieve was already up, sitting in a chair, looking out at the water. It is a lovely view. She told me that was the first time she had been out of that bed for days and it felt good to be up. She ate a little bit of Cream of Wheat, which she said wasn't too bad. Who would have ever thought my sister would have anything good to say about hospital food? What I want to say to you, Sara, or actually I would like to share with you, is our conversation. I hope that it might bring you some clarity to the life that you and your sister and brothers have had, and for you in particular, perhaps some closure."

I turn off the ignition, roll down the window for air, and listen as my aunt tells me a story.

"Sara, your mother and father were destined to be together, but only God knows why. They came from entirely different backgrounds. We—Genevieve and I—came from the upper-middle class, your father's family were hardworking blue-collar people. There isn't anything wrong with this difference, but in your parents' case, the writing was on the wall. Your father was a brilliant, sensitive man. I believe he preferred to be alone, reading, spending time in nature, or for a time there, being with you kids."

This is where I want to interrupt and say, well, he didn't do a very good job at being with his kids. Instead, I just sit and listen.

"When we were growing up, Genevieve and I spent our time going to school, shopping, being with our friends, and, of course, we spent the summers on the beach. Meme and Pops kept us busy with golf and tennis lessons, and for Genevieve, riding lessons. Michael's life was different. He and his brothers worked after school to help pay for their tuition. Did you know that all three Austin boys went to prestigious high schools in the city?" *Yes, I did know that.* "It is rather astonishing that the family could afford to do that. That is a testament to your grandfather's determination to be sure to see to it that his boys got the best education available to them. Sara, they were a good family."

None of this is news to me but I let Emma continue.

"You may be shocked to know that your mother was a bit of a handful growing up," Emma says with just a bit of sarcasm in her tone. "She drove our parents crazy. It was always something with Genevieve. She told me she was reminiscing lately, thinking back to when she first met Michael. It was at a school dance. She was enrolled in a junior college then, majoring in Business Administration, but excelling in horsemanship, which to our parents' annoyance was not a major, just an extra expense that Genevieve had to have. She thought Michael was handsome, and he certainly was, not too tall, about six feet, but my god, those blue eyes, his dark hair, and a smile that lit up the room. She actually wondered if his smile was better than hers. Can you believe that? Of course you can, she's your mother. Genevieve was nineteen years old, away from our parents, a rebel as a child, and now she was a rebel in college, on her own—look out, world! Your parents flirted, did the dance that was expected in those days. Genevieve was glowing, reminding me about her glory days. Their first date was disastrous for Michael, exhilarating for Genevieve."

"Why was it a disaster for Dad?" I ask, wondering if I am opening up a can of worms with Emma.

"I'm getting to that, dear," Emma said, and then continued. "Your mother invited Michael to her school to spend an afternoon together. I am sure that Michael had hoped for something a bit more intimate, or at least something a bit tamer than what it turned out to be. Genevieve told me that she remembers bringing Michael to the stables. She had it all planned. In those days she was intoxicated by the smell in the barn. The sweetest sound to Genevieve was the snorts and whinnies of the horses. The stomping of their hooves. The best touch in the world was a horse's velvet muzzle, the tickle of their whiskers.

And, of course, she looked amazing in her formfitting jodhpurs and expensive riding boots. 'How could he not have been impressed with me?' Genevieve said to me. Your mother was five-eleven, thin, athletic, remarkably beautiful, and she carried herself with poise and self-assurance, which could be a bit intimidating. Sara, it was as if she was back to her nineteen-year-old self telling me this story."

I'm getting annoyed with Emma. I don't need to be reminded of my mother's beauty and confidence. It's just another benchmark that I will never reach.

"But I digress. Genevieve said she saddled up the horses with an air of confidence that Michael had never seen. He never said that, but your mother said she certainly knew it. She helped him on his horse, instructed him on the basics, knees in, heels down, elbows in, sit up straight, but most important of all, be gentle on the bit. They started out slowly, of course, that was the responsible thing to do. As soon as Genevieve got them to a wide-open path, she let loose, kicked her horse into gear, looked back at Michael, and shouted, 'Let's go!' Well, go they went. Michael did okay, but he wasn't in her league. Genevieve told me she knew it at that moment, but she didn't let up. She took a turn off the groomed trail. 'Let's see what he's got,' she said she was thinking. They were at a fast canter when they came around a bend, Genevieve said she yelled, 'Duck,' as she and her horse barely made it around a leaning tree. Michael didn't hear her. Michael didn't duck. His horse went one way, and your father flew off the horse and hit the tree.

"I think that if your father had any sense, he would have dusted off his pants, never to be seen again. But he didn't. He got back on the horse and chased after her down the trail. Michael Austin was determined to embrace Genevieve's world. No matter that he could never live up to her expectations."

"I'm glad you and Genevieve had such a pleasant walk down memory lane," I say. I'm not sure what to make of this story and I don't want to upset or make my aunt feel that she shouldn't have revealed their private conversation.

"I have just a bit more to tell you, dear. This is what I hope will help you in the days to come. Sara, your mother is not afraid to die. She is at peace with the inevitable. What is it our father used to say? *'Not too much you can do about it darlin'.'*

"Genevieve said to me, 'Who would have thought that Sara would have become my anchor, my advocate?' It has not escaped your mother what you are doing for her. Sara, you have been so strong. I never thought our free-spirited Sara had this in her. Those are my words, dear, not your mother's. She also said that you and the others get that strength from her. I think she's right. You are all resilient people, and you have all done so well, despite what life gave you at a young age. But just when I thought your mother was doing penance, reviewing some of the errors of her ways, she said, 'Damn that Michael, damn him to hell. I did the best that I could with those kids considering the hand I was dealt with.'

"Some things never change, Sara, least of all your mother. I need to run, dear, I don't want to be late for church."

We hang up, and I sit in my car in my driveway, trying to digest the conversation Emma and I just had. I'm not sure what to think. What was Emma's reason for telling me all that? Although I hadn't known how my parents met, so that's interesting. But what am I supposed to do with this out-of-the-blue exposé on my parents? I want to take some time to process what Emma told me, but right now I need to snap out of it and drive to the hospital, which I can probably do with my eyes closed at this point. That might be a good thing because Emma's call has rattled me.

The hospital parking lot is full. Must be because it's Sunday, I think as I pull into a space further away than I like. It's cold, another gray, blustery February day in New-port. The wind is whipping off the harbor—not a day to make one feel a lot of hope.

I stay in my car for a few minutes. I'm not ready to put on my happy face for anyone. I think about Genevieve, my dad, and what Emma said about them.

It's cold in the car, a bit like my heart at the moment. Time to go see Genevieve. I take a deep breath, get out of the car, and follow the route to her room.

"Hi, Mom."

"Oh, Sara, I didn't expect you to come in today. Why aren't you home with your husband? You do still have a husband, right?"

"Yes, I still have a husband. How are you feeling? You look good," I say as I bend down to kiss her.

"I feel so much better. The procedure, whatever the hell it's called, has relieved so much pressure on my stomach. I even ate a bit this morning. I think it's time I go home. I just don't know if that is possible. I suppose I could go to the rehab place and get stronger and then go home. I am feeling overwhelmed, which is not like me. I certainly do not like feeling this way."

"Well, I'm glad you're feeling better. Of course you're

overwhelmed, this is all so much to take in. But I do have some news for you that you aren't going to believe. An actual doctor called me on Saturday. Dr. Cook, you remember Dr. Cook, right?"

"Of course I do," she snapped. "My body might be going but my mind is as sharp as ever. What did he have to say, and I wonder why he didn't come to me?"

"I don't think he was actually here in the hospital when he called and probably felt it was easier to talk to me on the phone rather than to try to call you here, you know, there are so many interruptions, nurses in and out, that might be why." I have always been able to come up with an excuse, lie, coverup—call it what you like, but I am quick on my feet.

"Maybe." Genevieve sounded doubtful. "What did he have to say?"

"Not a lot, other than you did really well with the procedure, and they took quite a bit of fluid out of your belly. He said that should relieve a lot of your discomfort."

"Well, he is right about that. I do feel so much better, but that doesn't tell me anything."

"No, Mom, it doesn't. Now we just need to wait for the results."

"That's the name of the game, sit around and wait. Sara, please go home, I am tired and want to rest. I also don't want to be the cause of your divorce."

"Okay, you win." I kiss my mother goodbye, grateful for a break from sitting in her hospital room. "See you tomorrow, Genevieve."

I take the robotic walk to the elevators, step inside, and watch the doors close in front of me. I am close to being done, burnt out, fried—whatever it's called, that's me.

I am such a tumble of emotions; my brain is on overdrive and Emma's call is still rattling my senses.

I would like to say I'm feeling nostalgic, maybe a bit melancholy, but to be completely truthful, I don't know what the fuck I'm feeling right now. As I go down the three floors to the main lobby of the hospital, I wonder what drew my parents together, to marry, to have four children? What the hell were they thinking? I cannot stop thinking about my life, who I am, where I belong in this world, this family, these Austins. I think both of my parents broke my heart, at times my will, and yet they are still my parents. Even at my age, I can't shake my upbringing—it's my foundation; it's who I am.

I get out of the elevator, go out the front door of the hospital to my car.

I sit in my cold car, waiting for the heat to crank up, and I think about my dad. I remember the one time when my grandmother Rose and I had tea. I was about eighteen. Growing up, we didn't spend much time with my father's parents, Rose and William. Genevieve had said it was because they lived so far from us. They lived in Brooklyn, so that was a poor excuse since we were only a train ride away. This particular day Rose had invited me to come for a visit, just me. I took the train into the city, got on the line 5 subway, and then walked the three blocks to her house.

At that point, Dad was more out of our family than in our family. We might go months without hearing from him. But once again, not at all out of character for him. This is what we grew up with.

I remember sitting in Rose's living room, waiting for her to finish making the tea. I had offered to help, but she told me to sit and relax. I felt like a guest, rather than a granddaughter visiting with her grandmother. If I were at Meme's house, she would insist that I help her out. She'd probably offer me a glass of champagne, instead of tea. Rose and Meme were polar opposites. Meme was tall and thin and was always dressed in the height of fashion; although, I don't recall ever seeing her in a miniskirt. Her hair, which was a beautiful shade of silver, was always perfect, the same as her makeup. She was never overdone, but Meme was definitely someone that got noticed.

Rose was also tall, but she was on the heavy side. I'd describe her as sturdy. She always wore her gray hair in a tight bun at the back of her head. Rose had beautiful skin and barely wore makeup. Maybe a bit of powder, but that was about it. She did, however, have a deep line between her brows making her appear stern, which she really wasn't. I had asked Genevieve about that when I was little. She told me that's a worry line, so I figured that Rose must always be worried. Rose didn't dress at all like Meme. I never saw her in shorts or a bathing suit. She was always in a dress, usually with an apron, when we would visit. She never wore any bright colors. Instead, her dresses seemed dark and old-fashioned to me, and her shoes were always black with thick soles.

After she poured the tea, Rose straightened her apron on her lap, cleared her throat, and said, "Sara, I think it's time I set the record straight about your father."

"I would love that, I know so little about him. What was he like growing up? Did he get along with his brothers? Was he a good kid, or a troublemaker? How did he do in school? Tell me everything." I was so eager to finally get some insight into my elusive father. It didn't matter why she chose to tell me now, I just wanted to hear everything.

Rose took a sip of tea and said, "Michael was a sweet little boy; he adored his older brothers and would follow them around like a puppy."

My father grew up in a large three-family walkup, on the top floor. It had four bedrooms, which were next to each other down a long hall, with one shared bathroom at the end. The hall floor was so highly polished that when we were little, we would take off our shoes and slide up and down on it. On the other side of the hall was the living room, which connected to the big dining room that opened to the massive kitchen and pantry. Off the back of the kitchen was a porch, where Rose would hang the clothes out to dry. The view from the porch was a circle of apartment buildings identical to where my grandparents raised their three boys. You could look out and see everyone's clothes hanging and look down three floors to a paved courtyard where kids would play basketball.

"I never noticed anything different in him other than he was quieter than his brothers. As he got older, I realized he loved to read, and he loved to write stories. William and I encouraged this. Herbert and Albert were much more active. They preferred being on the basketball court to reading a book. But all three of my boys were so smart. Al went to Annapolis on a scholarship, and Herb the Naval Academy, also on a scholarship. Michael was awarded one to Harvard early in his senior year at Trinity. He just needed to make it through that year, and he was on his way to Harvard and who knew what amazing opportunities would come his way. But all that changed. A single phone call and our lives were turned upside down."

Rose took another sip of her tea; her hand was shaking and she had tears in her eyes. I knew what was coming but

I let her continue. I could see that, after all these years, Rose was still in pain.

"My darling Albert, my firstborn, died in an automobile accident on Christmas Eve. He was only twenty-two years old. He was a passenger; the driver had been drinking. I didn't handle it well. But who's to say how you are supposed to handle the death of your child? I withdrew from the family I had left. William started to put in longer hours at work, Herb went back to the Academy after the funeral. The hole in our family, the changes in our structure, left Michael on his own. A seventeen-year-old boy needs supervision and guidance; we provided him neither in his senior year. We, or at least I, knew that he was drinking when he was out with friends. He had put down his books and picked up a bottle. I always stayed awake to be sure he came home. I would hear him trip on the stairs, stagger down the hall. He still got up, went to school, and got good grades. But on weekends, he would disappear, coming home Sunday evening disheveled, hungover, reeking of alcohol. It was a tough time for all of us, and I wish I had been a stronger person. I wish I had shaken him, slapped some sense into him, but I didn't. Instead, I used my grief as an excuse to ignore him. I was not a good mother in those days. The only thing I could focus on was Michael going to Harvard. I was sure that he would straighten up at Harvard. But that didn't happen. At the end of his senior year, one week after graduation, your father enlisted in the Air Force and gave up his scholarship. William and I were devastated. This is not what we wanted for our youngest child. But what was done, was done. I'm not sure why your father started drinking. Oh, sure, I know that boys will be boys. But I also know that most boys grow out of that stage, they can control their alcohol, they don't need to get drunk. That never happened with Michael. After your parents were married, which surprised your grandfather and me, and after he was discharged from the service, Michael seemed to be the person I knew him to be. I thought the three years he spent in the Air Force had brought my son back to reality. I think that it was easier for William and me to ignore the writing on the wall. We were wrong. We were so very wrong."

"Rose, why were you surprised that they got married?" I felt so sad for this woman, my father's mother, but the mention of my mother intrigued me.

"It was unexpected, at least to me. We had met Genevieve a few weeks before Michael left for basic training in the summer of 1942. They had met at a dance earlier in the year and it looked to me like they had taken to each other immediately. Genevieve had already completed her first year of college, which was another surprise for us. Nowadays, it's not so unusual for the woman to be older than the man, but in those days, it was definitely not the norm. But we liked her quite a bit. She was charming and seemed quite sure of herself, but not in a standoffish sort of way. Personally, I didn't think it would last. They were young, and he was going off to war. But war does funny things to people. They married when he came home on leave before he went off to Germany. Would you like more tea, dear?"

"No, thank you, but I will have another cookie," I said, hoping that it wasn't the end of Rose's story. Fortunately, it wasn't.

"Sara, I love my son, but I am not equipped to handle

his disappearances. I cannot condone how he neglected Genevieve, how he neglected his own children. But there was no talking to him then, and sadly there is no talking to him now. Years after William died, Michael was diagnosed with alcoholism. I'm not sure why we needed to hear that, to label him as an alcoholic, but I suppose it gave me some peace to understand that alcoholism is a disease, and my son suffers from this disease. He is a man who should never have picked up that bottle, and he hasn't been strong enough to completely stop drinking for his family. I'm afraid that this disease is going to kill him."

I remember sitting next to Rose on her floral couch, the tea now cold. I didn't know what to say. I was young and insensitive to what she just told me.

I wanted to say, "Well, too bad for Dad. I loved him, depended on him, and he just let me down, didn't give a rat's ass about me. What about Jessica? What about her having to drive Dad home because he was too drunk to drive? What about Parker, waiting at Penn Station, just a kid, and his father is a no-show? Or Ray? What about him? He barely remembers Dad." But I didn't say any of that. I needed more information from Rose.

"Rose, I understand that alcoholism is a disease, but I don't understand why he couldn't stop drinking. He was sober for the first five or six years of my life. If he could do that, why can't he stop again?"

"Sara, you were too young to realize that your father wasn't always sober then. William and I were at your house for your third birthday. Michael never showed up. You were such a little thing, so incredibly sad. You wanted your father, nobody else, just him. It was a cold winter day and I remember you sitting on the wall by the driveway waiting for him to come home. Mrs. Lemaire, Meme, went and sat with you. She was the only one who could talk to you. You just sat out there, in the cold, refusing to budge until your father came home. I'm not sure what made you change your mind—either you got too cold, or Meme convinced you to come inside. My heart broke for you that day."

"I don't remember that," I said quietly. I felt so sad for that little girl.

"It's probably just as well that you don't. I think it's easier to remember the good times with your father."

"But did they ever love each other? Did Genevieve and Dad ever love each other?"

Rose was quiet, probably thinking about how to carefully choose her words. "I'm sure they did love each other at one time. But I think if they had waited, if the war, circumstances, hadn't pushed them into a hasty marriage, the relationship would have run its course. But you cannot rewrite history, dear."

"I know that you can't, and I know that my childhood memories are fuzzy, to say the least. But I do remember my parents doing nice things together. Before Parker and Ray were born, I remember going to the tennis courts with them. They played and I sat at a picnic table watching them. Even then I sensed that they were such a beautiful couple to watch. I can remember us being at Meme and Pops' house in the summer. Dad would take us to the beach, we'd get ice cream after dinner. I remember when Dad surprised Genevieve with a brand-new convertible. Rose, I do remember a lot of good times." But as I spoke, different memories were coming forward, memories I had hidden away, memories that I wasn't aware of. Yes, he did surprise Genevieve with the convertible, but instead of being excited or happy, Genevieve started yelling at him in the driveway. She was berating him for buying a car without discussing it with her. "How could you do this, Michael? We can't afford this."

I remembered coming home from a Sunday morning riding lesson and Dad was there. I was young, maybe six. Genevieve was annoyed that he was there, but I didn't understand why. He asked me if I wanted to spend the day with him. I was thrilled; just me and Dad together for the day. I went running up the stairs to change. But then I remembered Genevieve screaming at him, "You are not taking her with you, Michael. You can't be trusted."

My mind was bringing up memories of my mother's anger, her rage. I could feel how scared I got; I could see myself hiding in my bedroom closet. I had shut the door, but I could still hear them arguing. Even then, as a six-year-old child, I knew that my father would leave without me. Even at six, I knew that he couldn't stand up to Genevieve.

I heard her come up the stairs. "Sara Austin, where are you? Sara?" She opened up the closet door. I was on the floor, huddled in a ball, terrified. "Get out of there. Get up, come out of there, right now." Of course, I did as she said. She looked me straight in the eye and said, "Sara Austin, you are the most ungrateful child on this earth. I spend half my morning watching you ride a horse in circles around a ring and yet you would rather be with your father. Go get cleaned up."

I wonder if that was when I began my retreat into my own world. Was that when I discovered how to disappear with the tides? Or was it when I was even younger, too young for me to pull up those memories?

"But Rose, honestly, what about when they were first married, when Dad came home from the war?" I couldn't let this go. I desperately needed to hear at least one positive word about my parents' marriage. Inside my head I was screaming—was the whole thing just one fucking mistake, and were Jess, Parker, Ray, and I a part of that mistake?

"Of course, dear, they were happy when Michael first came home. The whole country was happy, the war was over. It was time for everyone to get back to life as they knew it. But this world is a harsh place for people like Michael. He had confided in Herb that when he was stationed in Germany, he found that the drinking made what was happening when his plane dropped bombs on the unknown targets below almost acceptable. For Michael, the alcohol made him numb to the horrors of the war."

"What do you mean, people like Michael?" I asked.

"Michael is an extremely sensitive person, someone who struggles with pretty much anything unpleasant. He avoids conflict at any cost, hides his emotions, and uses alcohol to help him cope. At least that is what one of his many doctors told me.

"By the time Michael came home, Genevieve had been living in an apartment in New Haven. After she graduated, she found a good job as a receptionist in a large downtown doctor's office. I'm not sure if you knew that or not."

I shook my head no; I didn't know any of this.

"I'm surprised you didn't know that. In retrospect, it could appear that Genevieve had begun her married life as if she were single. I knew it was hard for Michael to move into the apartment, to feel comfortable. It seemed to be her home; he felt like a guest. He was twenty-three years old when he got in his first car accident because he was drinking. He was already married. He'd been to war, he was expected to act like everything was ok, and now there was a baby on the way. I will never talk poorly about Genevieve—after all, she is the mother of my grand-children, but I think that Genevieve felt that she had married beneath her station. She did tell me one afternoon how disappointed she was with Michael, how he never rose in the ranks in the Air Force. She compared him to her friends' husbands, fiancés. They had each gone into the service as a private and come home as a captain. But in Genevieve's defense, I think that she was given too much to deal with at such a young age. She was becoming resentful with the restrictions of being married and then when she found out she was pregnant...personally, I think that she felt trapped. In those days divorce was unheard of, dear. Your parents are—or at least were—Catholics. Divorce wasn't an option. In those days people stuck it out. They had more children and did what they felt was expected of them. I believe your father's drinking and his disappearances pushed your mother to the brink, es-pecially since they didn't have a strong foundation to begin with. I can't blame her, she put up with a lot. I can't tell you how many times Michael had to be picked up from jail, how many cars he crashed, how many jobs he lost. And add four kids to the mix. If it weren't for her parents, I don't know what would have happened to your family."

"I don't understand. What did Meme and Pops do for us?" I was getting more and more confused and annoyed.

"Mr. Lemaire, Pops, did all he could to help Michael. I

know that he liked Michael, but he didn't like that he had to bail him out of all of his indiscretions. It was Edward who got Michael the job with the electric company. Your father did his best in those years, maybe that's the father you remember. He did well with the company, became head of their union. Life seemed to be finally working out for your parents. I'm not sure what went wrong, probably not just one event. But knowing now that he was, is, an alcoholic, it seemed that sobriety was not something he could manage. Maybe he was trying to keep up to your mother's standards, maybe it was the responsibility of four children, a mortgage, and a wife who demanded a lot from him, but that's no excuse for what your father did."

I was caught by surprise. What did he do that I didn't already know about?

Rose paused as if she needed to catch her breath. She looked out the apartment window and then turned back to me and continued, "When Michael was caught stealing from the union dues, Pops paid back the money. Michael was fired. Soon after that, he was admitted to a Veterans' hospital to get sober. He was there for months."

While Rose talked, I was thinking, what the hell? Why did this all have to fall on Pops, when it's your son who's such a loser?

I sat next to this woman, my grandmother, who had just dumped a lifetime of family history on my lap. I didn't say anything for what seemed like forever, but then I held Rose's wrinkled, cold hand, and smiled at her. "Rose, I know this was a hard conversation to have with me. It was hard to hear, but also it's something that I needed to hear, and I guess you felt the same way. Otherwise, we wouldn't be sitting here together. Thank you so much for filling me in on some of my family history, an insight into my father, my parents, and their marriage. I should probably get going. I think it would be awkward for all of us if Dad came in and asked what was going on."

I thanked her for the tea and cookies and gave her a kiss on the cheek. I never saw Rose again.

The ring of my cell phone brings me back to reality, shakes me out of my unpleasant walk down memory lane.

"Hi, any updates on Genevieve?"

"I'm worried about you," Jess says after I fill her in on the call with the doctor and how much better Genevieve seems to be today.

"Why? I'm fine." Not sure why, but I haven't told anyone about my conversation with Emma this morning. Not Keith, Liza, or Jessica.

"But you're doing all of this on your own. You're the only one at the hospital advocating for Genevieve, running interference with her visitors, and trying to work, all the same time."

You're right, Jess, this is tough. Genevieve is tough, work is tough. God, I'm tired. But I don't say that to my sister. Instead it's the usual, "Oh, I'm fine, don't worry about me. Other than I think I lost five pounds this week, ha-ha." In reality, I do think that all of this stress has resulted in a bit of weight loss. I guess that's my silver lining.

DAY EIGHT

"You only live once, but if you do it right, once is enough."
– Mae West

Is the sun ever going to come out, I wonder as I unpack my laptop, plug it in, punch in the hospital password that I have finally memorized, and look over at my sleeping mother. I can't believe that I'm back here, another Monday. How many days have I been in this hospital? Eight days. Genevieve has been here for twelve days. This is nuts.

She is just starting to wake up, and I can tell that she looks so much better. Her color is brighter; she has improved even since yesterday.

"Oh, is that you, Sara?" Genevieve asks, waking up just in time for a nurse's aide to come in.

"Good morning, Genevieve. My name is Leslie and I'm just going to check your vitals. How was your night?"

"Every day it's someone new." Genevieve seems to be adjusting to life in the hospital. I'm not sure if that's a good thing or a bad thing. I say, for now, it's a good thing.

"I know, it can get a bit confusing with all of us coming and going. Your blood pressure is a bit low. I'll put that in your chart, so your doctor is aware."

Leslie finishes up her tasks and before leaving the room, she says, "I hope you don't mind me saying this, but you are the talk of this floor. Nobody can believe you're ninety-four. Nobody—and we've all seen a lot of patients. You take care and have a good day."

Genevieve smiles. "Why would I mind hearing that, Leslie? I know I don't look a day over eighty."

Well, that should keep her happy for a while, I think, getting back to work.

I work and Mom dozes; we seem to have this routine down, I think, just as two doctors come in.

"Good morning, Genevieve, and you must be Sara." A young woman puts her hand out to me, and then to Genevieve, who has woken up again.

"I am Dr. Jennifer Sampson, and this is my colleague Dr. Andrew Jones. We are today's morning rounds team and have spent some time going over your case. You have been here for quite some time."

"Twelve days. Today is day twelve." I am trying to control my tone.

"Genevieve, the results of the paracentesis have come in."

Genevieve sits up a bit straighter, and I actually stand up, notebook in hand, and go to the end of my mother's bed.

"I am sorry to say that we have discovered advanced gastric adenocarcinoma."

There it is, I think, the C-word, just disguised as "adenocarcinoma." As soon as these words come out of the doctor's mouth, my mother and I lock eyes. We don't move our heads, we don't shift our bodies, we just look; we seem to look into each other's souls. It is a look that will stay with me for the rest of my life.

A look between a daughter and mother

A look between a mother and daughter.

A look that crosses eternity and strengthens an unknown bond between us. A look that shows compassion, fear, worry, safety, relief. It is a look of pure, sheer love. I am overwhelmed, not by the news so much, but by the silent communication that passes between my mother and me.

"I'm terribly sorry," Dr. Jones says. He really does look sorry.

"Well, well, I never planned on this," Genevieve says, straightening her blanket.

"Yes, this is news that no one wants to hear. You said that you had a plan?" Dr. Sampson asks in a quiet and respectful tone.

"My plan was a stroke, and that would be the end of it. How long do I have?" Genevieve sounds exceedingly composed, especially for having just been told she has cancer.

"That's difficult to say. Perhaps two to three months with intervention."

"So, where do we go from here?" Genevieve asks.

Both doctors glance at each other. Dr. Jones responds, "There are definitely options for you to consider. You can go to a nursing facility where you would have round-the-clock care, and they would help to get you stronger, more ambulatory. Or you can go home, also with round-the-clock private care. Either of these options will require that you return to the hospital by ambulance on a weekly basis to undergo a paracentesis procedure, which will keep you comfortable, relieve the bloating, digestive issues, the pain, all of which will return. These symptoms are going

to return, Genevieve. The cancer is getting more aggress-
ive, the fluids are going to return, along with the pain and
discomfort."

"Why would I do either of those options?"

"We can consider surgery and chemo. Something I
wouldn't recommend for anyone your age and considering
the progression of the cancer," says Dr. Sampson.

I am frozen, not sure what to say or do, but I sure as
hell will not break down, not now, not yet. No outgoing
tide for me. Soon, but not now.

Genevieve raises her right hand which tugs a bit on the
intravenous needles in her right hand.

"When I asked where we go from here, I was asking
how I can die." She is calm, speaking clearly; this is her
life, her choice.

Dr. Sampson stumbles on her words, taken aback for
just a second. "Massachusetts is not a right-to-die state.
We can discuss hospice as an option."

"Oh dear, this is a bit of a disappointment. I was
hoping to move to the Ritz and spend my last days in
luxury, being waited on hand and foot. But never mind
that, let's discuss hospice."

I'm sure that Dr. Sampson is grateful to move onto a
conversation that she is comfortable with. She explains,
"The hospice team provides medical care and support
services to the patient and to the patient's family and
friends. Hospice doesn't attempt to cure, but rather to
control pain and other symptoms in order to enable you to
live as fully and comfortably as possible. Would you like
me to arrange to have a hospice worker come and speak
with you and your daughter first thing in the morning?"

Genevieve agrees to meet with hospice, and just like

that, things seem to be coming to a screeching halt.

Damn it, I am fighting back tears as the doctors leave. Genevieve looks small; she has never looked small to me, to us, to anyone.

"Sara, dear." Genevieve smiles and holds out her hand to me.

"Oh, Mom," I say as I take her hand. "Oh, Mom. This just sucks."

"Yes, it does, and you know I hate that word."

We sit together quietly, each of us trying to digest what just happened.

Finally, Genevieve speaks up. "This doesn't surprise me, Sara, this diagnosis. I have felt for months that I have cancer, but that damn Dr. Masterson wouldn't listen to me. Not that that matters much now. But what I need to say to you is this. I'm worried. Sara, I am worried about you kids after I'm gone."

"Mom, they said you could have two to three months; it could be longer."

"I left so many things unfinished, the guest room closet is a mess of paperwork," she says as if she didn't hear me.

"If that's what's got you worried, you can stop. I'm pretty sure we can clean out the guest room closet. You can sit there and direct us—actually, how about you just direct Parker on what to keep and what to throw out?"

"Oh, it's more than that. I want you all to get along, to behave like a family, not fight and bicker like you all do. I couldn't stand when you and your sister and Parker weren't talking, or that Ray stays away from everyone. I want you to promise me that you will stay a family. I want you to be alright."

"Mom, we are going to be alright." I am struggling to

keep my voice from cracking, to keep my tears at bay.

"Sara, promise me that you mean that."

"I promise."

Genevieve rests back on her pillow; she looks surprisingly serene considering the death sentence she just received.

"What is your happiest childhood memory? Be sure I'm in it."

I sigh. This could be difficult. There aren't many fond memories, at least of my mother.

"I think it would be the very first time I rode a horse. Not a pony, but a horse. I can remember it so clearly. I felt like I was on top of the world."

"Oh, yes, I remember that. You were about five years old, and that damn horse was the size of a Clydesdale. You were a peanut on top of him. That's why you felt like you were on top of the world. Do you remember how his nose kept running down my arm the whole time I was leading you around the ring?"

"I do, I thought he had a bad cold. I felt bad for him. But do you remember what happened?"

Genevieve is quiet for a minute. "I let go of his lead while opening the gate and he took off for the barn with you hanging on. I was terrified that you were going to fall off or smash your head on the doorway into the barn."

"You were yelling, 'Hang on, Sara, hang on, duck!'" I can remember it like it was yesterday. It was a cold day, no sun. I was wearing a red jacket and my jodhpurs and riding boots; nobody wore helmets then. Genevieve led me around the ring and the horse's nose kept running down her arm. Around and around we went. "Sit up straight, Sara, remember to keep your knees in and your heels down. Be gentle with him, no matter what." When the lesson was finished, she let go of his lead to open the gate. The gate was barely open, but that giant horse had a mind of his own and went charging for the barn. I can still picture racing up the paved driveway to the barn, can still hear my mother yelling. I wasn't scared—I was exhilarated, clueless as to how badly that could have ended.

"But you hung on, kid, you did good, as Pops would say. You've been doing good your whole life, Sara. You have had some difficult times, but you always hung on, you always did good. I am so proud of you."

I'm struggling to keep the tears back. "Oh, Mom, thank you."

Once again, we sit quietly together, mother and daughter, each with our own thoughts, but I am quite sure she's wondering the same thing as I am—what's next?

"So, Mom, what's your favorite memory?" I ask, breaking the silence in her room.

Outside of room 3799, life goes on, phones ring, nurses hurry from room to room, carts roll by. Room 3799 is temporarily shut off from the world.

"That is a tough one. Let me think." I watch her lying back on her pillows. It seems that she is really putting some thought into this.

"I suppose my favorite memory is being seated between Henry Kissinger and Spiro Agnew at a dinner at the White House. I loved what I wore; it was an off-the-shoulder Oscar de la Renta fuchsia gown, remarkably simple, and extremely elegant. My hair looked amazing, and I had wonderful conversations with engaging, brilliant people. Oh, it was a night to remember, for sure."

I smile ruefully, shake my head. Wonderful, just wonderful, Mother. True Genevieve to the end.

Again, we sit silently together until Genevieve dozes off.

I get up and slowly walk to the family room to call my family. I guess I'm now going to use this room for what it is actually intended.

"Hi, Sara."

"Hey, Jess."

"How are you? How's Genevieve today?

"Jess, Mom has cancer, stomach cancer." These might be the hardest words I ever have to say, and I realize I just blurted them out. I offered no safety net for my sister to shield her from the harshness of our new reality, which is death. I just blurt it out.

Silence. I can hear my sister across the country take a deep breath. I wonder why Jess can take a deep breath and I can't.

"Oh dear, what does this mean?"

"Well, it means that Mom doesn't want any treatment, anything that will prolong her life. She wants to die. Jess, Mom wants to die."

"Oh, okay, okay, did they say how long before that happens?" I realize Jess couldn't bring herself to say the word—*die*. I just said it twice in one sentence. Die, Mom is going to die.

"Two to three months."

"So, what do we do?"

I explain the few options that we have and tell her about Genevieve shocking the doctor with her question about how to die. "Too bad Massachusetts isn't a right-to-die state."

"Well, California is a right-to-die state." Jess springs to

life. "I'll fly her out here and she can stay at our beach house in Santa Cruz. I have a friend who won a big lawsuit."

Where is this going, I wonder, collapsing into the hospital's family room couch.

"After he won the suit, and it was substantial, actually it was huge, he bought an enormous department store that had gone out of business. He gutted the place and turned it into a beautiful retirement village where the residents eventually transition into the assisted living part of the place. Imagine that? He told me that the families have their drugs shipped in from China and it's as easy as that."

"What kind of drugs?" I can't believe I am having this conversation.

"You know, the kind that speed things up, let you spend your last days pain-free, in peace, do it your way, not the medical way."

"I'll bring it up with Mom and see what she has to say." Okay, let's just add crazy to the family traits.

"Sara, you okay? I'm worried about you. You've been alone through this whole ordeal, dealing with Genevieve, which is an ordeal in itself."

"I don't know. This is surreal, sad, a relief, I just don't know. It's just really odd, that's the only way I can describe it. I need to call Parker and Liza. Will you please call Ray for me?"

"What should I say? We don't really know what the plans are yet. She could be coming out here, for all we know."

"Just tell him that, Jess. Just tell him that we don't know anything yet, other than Genevieve is dying," I say, exasperated.

"Okay, I'll call Ray. Let me know what she thinks about coming here. I'm going to start doing some research on those Chinese drugs. Bye."

"Bye."

I just want to disappear into the couch or run out the door and race to the harbor. I am so, so, so tired. Is this grief circling around my perimeter, ready to grab me like an octopus and bring me down? I need to call Parker.

"Hi, Sara."

"Hi, Parker. I'm sorry to say but it's time to come home. Genevieve's been diagnosed with cancer and she has only a few months to live."

"Oh shit, what kind?"

"Stomach." What I want to scream is, why does that matter? Our mother is dying. What does it matter what is killing her? She is going to die.

"Did you talk to her?"

"Of course I talked to her. I was with her," I say, annoyed. What a stupid question.

"No, I mean, did you talk to her?"

"Did I talk to her about what, Parker?"

"About why she's the way she is? Did you ask her if she has one maternal bone in her body? Did you ask her if she thinks she was a good mother? Sara, did you do any of this?"

"No, Parker, I didn't talk to her about any of that. I figured, with her dying and all, this probably isn't the best time to bring up her shortcomings as a mother." I knew exactly what Parker was asking me. But right then and there, in the family room of the Newport Hospital, I realize that my years of issues with my mother are gone. This time that I have spent in the hospital with her and this death sentence has grabbed hold of that shit, tossed it out the window, sent it to the harbor in the February wind, and drowned every last thing I thought I hated about my mother.

"I wish you had. I wish you would. Anyway, I'll give her a call. I'll let you know when we can change our tickets and get home ASAP. I need to cancel a lot of reservations, hotels, dinners; we had some tours booked and paid for." I hear Parker sigh; this must be hard for him being so far away. But I know my brother. He will do what he said he's going to do and come home.

The next call is going to be my hardest.

"Hi, Mom."

"Hi, honey. I have some news about Genevieve. We finally have a diagnosis."

"Oh?"

"Genevieve has stomach cancer. She's decided to not do any type of intervention. Even if she did try to extend the time she has, it wouldn't be a pleasant way for her to spend the last few months of her life. So, she's coming home and will start hospice care as soon as possible."

"Oh no, I don't know what to say."

"I know, honey. I know. You would think that we would all be prepared to lose Genevieve, but I don't think any of us are."

"When is she coming home?"

"I think tomorrow. I'll let you know as soon as I do. Parker and Jess are making arrangements to come home, too."

"Mom, this is so sad. I love you."

"It is sad, but it's somewhat of a relief to finally know what we're facing. I love you, too. Will you let Tess know, please? I'll let you figure out how you can tell Max."

I feel old, sitting in the family room of the hospital, trying to figure out what is next. What is next, Mom?

Ping. I look at my phone. Email from Beth.

Hey, Sara, I got your job description, please let me know how much time you spend on each of your tasks, get it to me by close of business today. Beth.

Breathe, Sara, breathe. Don't cry, Sara, don't cry. Stand up, Sara, stand up. Sara, Sara, Sara, take a step out the door, down the hall. Sara, do this: breathe, don't cry, stand, step. Sara, you can do this. Sometimes I hate that voice in my head, but I do as I'm told. I breathe, I don't cry, I stand, I step, I walk to room 3799 and deal with everything that I would prefer to run away from.

"Hey, Mom, I'm back."

We smile at each other. The air in the room is heavy. I can sense a shift. This time the shift is in Genevieve.

"I just talked to Jess," I say, hoping to lighten the air in the room.

"Oh dear, is she is terribly upset? Could you add some water to her flowers?"

"Sure, yes, of course she's upset. So, Jess suggested that you go and stay with her. What do you think of that idea?" I figured I would omit telling her about the Chinese drugs at this point.

"Oh, I can't travel. I understand her determination, but I just want to go home. It's awfully hard for your sister. She is so far away, she feels useless, and you know Jess, she needs to do everything, and she needs to do it her way, the right way."

"Okay, I agree. Then I guess we should talk about the option of using hospice at your house. I called Parker and they're coming home." I almost whispered the part about Parker. For some annoying reason, Genevieve hates intruding on her sons.

Surprisingly, she asks how soon before he is home, and what about Ray? She wants her kids home with her. I wonder if Genevieve feels defeated. Does she feel that this is the end? The actual end of her life. God, what must that feel like?

I rearrange the flowers from Jess. It is a very odd feeling, if odd is even the right word, to be in a room with someone who's dying, with someone who knows that she is going to die, sooner rather than later. What am I supposed to be doing right now? I am fairly sure the answer is not rearranging flowers. What should I feel? How should I act? We both know that she's dying, what the fuck am I supposed to do? What is she supposed to do? We have fought so many times throughout my life. I have run away from her more times than I can count. I have hated her—she has hurt me so deeply, so emotionally. I have hurt her, yet here I am standing in front of my mother's hospital bed, helpless.

"Mom, we are all going to be here for you."

"Sara, I want to rest. Please go home."

"I'll stay a bit longer, you rest."

What kind of a world is it, that a person is told their mother has two to three months to live, and less than an hour later that person has to go back to work? That kind of world is my world.

Now I need to lie, distort, fabricate, whatever you want to call it, but I need to do what Beth asked, which is the last thing I want to do right now. I want to lie down on the day bed with an IV of vodka and say fuck you, world.

138

Despite the unbelievably odd day I've had, I get through it. I'm on my way home when Jess calls.

"Sara, I need to talk to you. Do you have a minute?"

"I do. I'm driving home, what's up? Oh, but before you start, Genevieve doesn't feel that she is up to traveling. I didn't mention the Chinese drugs."

"Okay, I kind of figured that would be how she'd feel. But that isn't why I called." Jess takes a breath. "After we hung up, after you told me what you told me, well, I needed to take some time to let your news sink in. I know this shouldn't be a shock, she's ninety-four years old, but this is a shock. Is this really happening?"

I start to respond but before anything comes out of my mouth Jess continues, "Sara, don't say anything, let me talk. So, after we hung up, I just sat, thinking. Actually, I'm not sure what I was thinking. But I said, Jessica Austin, get off your ass and do what you do best."

"Okay, what did you do, Jess?" She is scaring me.

"Well, I started to research those Chinese drugs, which now I know was a waste of time. Anyway, I remembered I was supposed to call Ray. Do you think it's odd we always forget about him? I've always felt that he was like a cute pet Mom brought home, and then we all lost interest in him. You know, like when people get, I don't know, gerbils. That's it, Ray is like our forgotten gerbil."

Okay, welcome to Crazy Town. "Jess, let's get past the gerbil analogy...did you call Ray?"

"I did. Sara, I just don't know about him. I called, he answered. I didn't really say anything like 'Hey, how's it going, bro?' Not that I would actually say something like that. So, I just told him, Mom has cancer. She's got a few months left to live and she might be coming out here to stay with us. I didn't say anything about the Chinese drugs."

"So, what did he say?"

"Nothing. He said absolutely nothing. The only reason I knew that he hadn't hung up is because I could hear him smoking. I cannot believe he still has that filthy habit. Actually, it was probably a joint." My sister sounds like judgmental Genevieve.

"Okay, so what happened next?"

"I told him someone would be in touch to let him know where Genevieve might be over the next few weeks. I'm telling you, Sara, that boy has his own soundtrack to life."

"Is that it? You said someone would be in touch and you guys hung up?" I'm trying to understand how she could just leave it at that. Mom is dying, and someone will be in touch, bye.

"Yes. Oh, and then I asked Russ to open a 2015 Pinot so I could fill him in on what we are about to face with Mom."

I am beyond blown away by this conversation. There have been a few today that have stopped me in my tracks. I review. First was Emma telling me about my father's shortcomings, and that my mother is prepared to die. Oh, let's not forget conversation number two: my mother is definitely dying of cancer. Conversation number three centered around Parker wondering if I had told my mother why she doesn't win any Mother of the Year awards. Conversation number four: can we get drugs from China to kill our mother? And now conversation number five: Ray is a gerbil who smokes. It is amazing to me that I am not a heroin addict.

DAY NINE

"I am ready to meet my maker, but whether my maker is
prepared for the great ordeal of meeting me
is another matter."
– Winston Churchill

I arrive at the hospital at the same time as I have for the
last nine days, with my laptop bag on my shoulder and
a fake smile plastered on my face. The world must never
see us showing any weakness: no sadness, only confidence and self-assurance.

I didn't sleep much last night, despite the three glasses
of wine and Tylenol PM. I felt like a monster—a really
heavy monster—was standing on my shoulders, pushing
me down, trying to bend me, break my back. I've had this
monster visit many times since I was a little girl. Most of
the time I'm able to stand up straight and push the monster off. Today is no different—stand up, step up, Sara, this
is what you have to do. No monsters today, Sara Austin.

"Good morning, Mom."

At that moment two people come into the room.
Neither wear the usual white lab coats or scrubs that
basically all of the hospital staff wear. Aside from their
name tags they could just be two people stopping by to

visit, to say hello to Genevieve. But they aren't visitors; they aren't just stopping by.

"Hello, Genevieve. We're from hospice. This is Raj Sharma, and I'm Audrey Campbell. Dr. Dalton asked that we come and meet with you this morning."

Genevieve smiles and tries to raise the back of her bed to sit up, fumbling with the button. "It seems awfully early for you people to be here."

"Here, let me get that for you." Audrey smiles, a genuinely warm smile. The type of smile that makes you think that everything is going to be okay, everything is going to work out. "Is that better? Yes, it is a bit early, I apologize but both Raj and I wanted to get you started off in the best way possible."

"Yes, much better, thank you." Genevieve is doing her best to rise to the occasion to discuss her death with complete strangers first thing in the morning. She looks over to Raj. "What did you say your name is?" she asks.

Oh, no, here we go again.

"Raj, Raj Sharma, and it is very nice to meet you." Raj is tall and thin, dressed in khakis and a blue Oxford shirt. He has a sense of calmness and reassurance about him.

"Sharma...what type of name is that?"

Raj looks confused, not sure how to answer her question.

"Spell it for me, spell your last name."

I'm trying to figure out how to stop this conversation before my mother commits some act of discrimination that causes a lawsuit.

"S-H-A-R-M-A."

"Oh, Sharma. What nationality is that?"

"I am from India," Raj says, smiling with a little nod of

his head.

"India, that's nice. I have never been there. I've heard it's a beautiful country, but a bit overpopulated and the children are starving."

Audrey seems to take that as her cue. Maybe she has training in dealing with inappropriate, entitled old people. "Genevieve, we would like to spend some time with you and your daughter if this is a good time. We hope to develop a plan of care for you."

"I don't need any care; I'm going home to die." Genevieve says these words as if she was telling someone she was going out for a walk.

Audrey doesn't miss a beat, the words from my mother not seeming to shock her in any way.

"We understand and respect your decision, Genevieve. Raj and I would like to make this transition as easy as possible for you."

Dr. Dalton is the next to join our little group. "Excuse me, good morning. I was on the floor for a consultation and thought that I would stop by to answer questions, help in any way that I can. Genevieve, with your permission I would like to fill Raj and Audrey in on your decision to not seek medical care, considering your advanced condition." He turns his attention to Raj and Audrey.

"As you know, Genevieve has been diagnosed with advanced gastric adenocarcinoma. After going over the options that are available, Genevieve has decided that the best course for her is to return to her home, to be with her family, and to live as she has specified, which is detailed in her Personal Directive.

"Genevieve, as we discussed before, with this type of cancer your symptoms and pain are going to return. I agree that hospice is your best option. We'll start you on a small dosage of morphine and the hospice team will train your caregivers on how to administer it when you're home."

Audrey moves closer to Genevieve's bed and asks, "How familiar are you with hospice care, Genevieve?"

I'm standing at the side of my mother's bed, amazed at how calm she seems with all of this alien information. I feel like I'm standing outside of myself, watching a Sara Austin that I don't know. How can this Sara be in this room listening to people talk about her mother dying? How can this Sara be in this room and witness her mother discuss her end-of-life care? How can this Sara not start scream-ing, *Make it stop!* Because the other Sara Austin knows that both Saras can deal with this together.

"I have some idea of it, but please fill me in, since this is probably what I am going to be facing for however long I have."

Audrey goes on to explain, "Hospice is a special kind of care that focuses on the quality of life for people and their caregivers who are experiencing an advanced, life-limiting illness. Hospice provides compassionate care for people in the last phases of an incurable disease so that they may live as fully and comfortably as possible. Due to your par-ticular needs, as Dr. Dalton explained, we will instruct your caregivers, whether that's family members or pro-fessional outside help, on what they can do to keep you comfortable. Your symptoms will return, and some things can be put in place to keep those symptoms at bay. We suggest that you limit your food and fluid intake, at least in the beginning. That's not to say that you'll go hungry or thirsty, but we want to monitor your bowels to avoid abdominal pain and vomiting. We will also be instructing your caregivers on how to administer the morphine. The morphine will help with any anxiety, pain, or nausea you might experience. We will assign you a hospice care co-ordinator, who will be in touch later today to go over what you'll need in place before you arrive home."

Audrey turns and looks at me. "Shall I give her your phone number, Sara, to make the arrangements?"

"Sure," is my inadequate response. I'm numb.

"Do either of you have any questions, or shall we move forward with setting this in motion, Genevieve?"

"Yes, let's move forward. When can I go home?"

"I think we can have you discharged tomorrow," Dr. Dalton says, watching a nurse quietly administer the morphine into Genevieve's IV.

Dr. Dalton, Audrey, and Raj leave me with a packet of hospice information, along with a list of phone numbers for different contacts. I am overwhelmed and now alone with Genevieve.

"Sara, I'm tired. This is all quite a bit to take in. I would like to be alone, I want to rest, and I want you to go home. Are you sure you still have a husband?"

"Yes, Mom, I'm pretty sure I still have a husband," I say as I kiss Genevieve goodbye. I get why she wants to be alone. Right now, I want to be alone. This is really, really hard.

I smile at the nurses at the nurses' station and take the now robotic walk to the parking lot. I don't call anyone while driving home, although I know I need to let Liza know Genevieve won't be home until tomorrow. But not now, not yet. Wonder what today's tide is? I could really use an outgoing tide, Mom.

But I don't drift away; instead, I go home, walk into my kitchen, love my dogs, and put the kettle on for tea.

Just as I sit down, my phone rings. It's Mary Armstrong from hospice, calling to let me know that she has ordered a hospital bed and hospital tray, which would be arriving at Genevieve's this afternoon. I remember that the Ms had said to let them know if I needed something. Well, I do—they can let the delivery people in and show them where to put Genevieve's beautiful queen-size bed in her garage. Genevieve is not going to be happy with any of this. I'll just tell her it was the Ms' fault.

I sip my tea and think about my siblings. What are they doing, thinking, feeling?

For better or worse, my family is coming home. They each emailed me and let me know their flights are booked and they are traveling tonight. They were able to get a bereavement fare, and they're headed to their different airports. The Austins are coming home. All but Ray. He didn't email or call, so I have no idea what he's doing. I wonder if he's feeling left out, overlooked, ignored in what we are all going to have to face. I imagine he would be pretty pissed off after being told his mother has two or three months to live and that someone would be in touch. I spend the afternoon pretending to work, pushing aside the inevitable that is coming at me like another fucking tsunami.

Keith comes home just after six, surprised to find me home.

"Not that I don't love that you're home, baby, but what's going on?" he asks, giving me a kiss.

Over a perfect martini, I fill him in on Genevieve's diagnosis, her plans for the next few months, and that my siblings are coming home. I fill him on everything other than how my heart is breaking.

It's late, I'm tired; *ping*, an email on my phone. This better not be work. Actually, it's an email from Parker.

Hi, we just boarded. Fortunately, first class still has Wi-Fi operating. Couple of things. What exactly are we coming home to? You said Mom has a few months to live. Are those going to be good months? Can she get around? Has anyone thought of what type of care we might need to get for her? Since you two seem to have reached a détente, I think that you are in the best position to talk to her about why she is the way she is. I know that you aren't one to embrace what could be an uncomfortable discussion, but it's time for us to get this out on the table. Strike while the iron is hot and start this conversation. I will be there as soon as I can, and I'll pick up where you leave off. At the very least Genevieve owes us an explanation and an apology. For now, Parker

I read his email twice. Seriously, Parker. You deal with Genevieve yourself. I'm not paving the way for you.

I hit delete and finish my drink, thinking, yeah, right now Parker is probably listening to a Tony Robbins or some other motivational podcast. But to be fair, I know that Parker is in pain—we all are. But the difference between my brother and me is that I don't hold a grudge, because I don't feel that solves anything. Parker's grudge against Genevieve goes back to his childhood. He wants her to apologize for all the alleged sins she committed.

COMING HOME

"On Wednesday, when the sky is blue, and I have nothing else to do, I sometimes wonder if it's true that who is what and what is who."
– Winnie the Pooh

Eight a.m.

"Hi, where are you?"

"Hi, Jess, I'm almost to the hospital. Where are you?"

"At Genevieve's. I got in late last night or early this morning, whatever. This house is filthy. I've spent the last few hours cleaning bathrooms and throwing out food. I'll never understand why she wouldn't hire a cleaning person."

"God, I hope there wasn't food in the bathroom. Did you sleep?"

"Seriously, this place is filthy." Jess and I have two different views on the definition of filthy. "I thought that instead of coming to the hospital, I'll stay here, clean, make it nice for her, and then I'll make some chicken soup. And no, I didn't sleep. When I got here, it was still dark. I just sat in her driveway. I just sat there almost as if I were afraid to get out of the car and go into her house. I was thinking, Mom should be here, Mom is supposed to be here. This is just so hard; I don't know how I can do this."

"Yup, it is hard. You can do this. We can do this, and we have to do this. But why are you are going to make chicken soup?" We had made a pact that we wouldn't encourage Genevieve to eat. And I am in no state to try to help my sister with her feelings when I am trying to keep mine in check.

"I'm just doing it to make the house smell nice—it's winter, chicken soup for the soul."

"Okay, that does sound nice. I'll text you when we leave the hospital." Another typical Austin reaction to anything. Jess is hurting, I'm hurting and I'm pretty sure Genevieve is hurting, but let's all just move forward, no time for empathy towards each other. That is what we do as Austins.

It's another cold, gray day—a day that offers little joy. Once again the wind is whipping up from the harbor as I walk into the hospital, just like I have done for the last nine days. I smile at the receptionists, follow the same green line, take the elevator to the third floor, and stand outside of room 3799 for the last time. How the hell am I doing this?

"Good morning, Mom. You get to go home today. Imagine, fourteen days in this damn hospital, but on a positive note the nurses and doctors have been great."

"Oh, hello, dear. Come sit for a minute. You don't have to work, do you?"

"No, not today," I lie. I'm not quite sure how I'm going to get away with not working today. I can be available by phone, I can get emails, text messages; hopefully, nobody will know that I'm not sitting at my desk at home. I need this job. I—we—need the money, but my mother needs me.

I cannot screw this up.

"Sara, I need to say something. I would like you to listen and not interrupt."

Deep breath. God, I could use a deep breath right now. "Okay, I won't interrupt."

"I have done a hell of a number on you and I am truly sorry." Genevieve puts up her hand as she senses that I am going to interrupt. "I was naïve, selfish, so out of my league when it came to raising you. You were such an easy baby; all you did was sleep. Your sister and Parker were colicky, and Ray, well, at that point...well, never mind about that. Sara, you were such a lovely, happy little girl, and I think that your father and I knocked that out of you. I love you; I have always loved you and so did he. We just didn't show love well and we sure as hell didn't parent well. I feel that you were raised in benign neglect. In those days there were no self-help books on how to raise your kids properly. For this, I am terribly sorry, and I hope that you can understand and maybe even forgive me. These days that we have spent together have been so important to me. You have shown such courage, compassion, and, well, you have been my anchor. I don't know if I could have dealt with all of this without you. Thank you, Sara."

What does one do with this unexpected bundle of sentiment, so full of emotions, for both the one pouring her heart out and the one on the receiving end? I am really uncomfortable with this side of my mother. This is not Genevieve. I don't know how to react to this heart-opening conversation. My mother is dying of cancer so I can't very well say, *Too little too late, Mom*. I feel a calm wash over me. I look out at the harbor, hesitate for only a minute, then, without saying a word, walk over to my mother, to

Genevieve, the woman who has been a thorn in my side for longer than I care to remember. Fighting back tears, I bend over her, and let her pull me in, let her hold me, let her hug me. My mother has never hugged me like this. This is a good hug, this is genuine, this is love.

I take a breath, an actual deep breath, stand up, and, holding my mother's hand, say, "Let's get you ready to go home, Mom."

Two nurses come in, not quite as cheery as usual. They like Genevieve. She has been with them longer than most patients and they know she is going home to die.

I watch as they administer morphine into my mother's intravenous bag. I witness the beginning of the end.

I leave her room and walk through the parking lot, pushing a wheelchair piled high with bags of Genevieve's numerous beauty products, her clothes, and a couple of extra sets of hospital sheets for the hospital bed. I'm also carrying my sister's vase of dying flowers. Rather fitting tribute to this moment. Genevieve insisted the flowers weren't that great anymore, but they are much too nice to leave for the nurses. Genevieve will arrive in about an hour by ambulance. She is coming home to die.

I load up the car with my mother's belongings, return the wheelchair to reception—this is obviously not like leaving your shopping cart in the lot—and try to figure out how to keep the stupid vase full of water from tipping over. In the big picture, this is the least of my concerns. Dead flowers spilling onto the car mat, a dying mother coming home.

I get in the car, shut the door, and try to breathe. This is it, I think, this is real, Mom is coming home to die. I put my head against the steering wheel and go over these last nine days of being in the hospital with Genevieve, nine days of a roller coaster of emotions.

Why was I at the hospital every day to be with Genevieve? Was it out of duty, obligation, or was it out of love? There are so many unpleasant memories for me, all the hurtful words Genevieve would throw at me, making me feel inadequate and, worse, unwanted. But I think something has shifted in both of us in these nine days. I understand just how fortunate I am to have had this time alone with my mother, other than a few dozen hospital workers who were part of the daily routine. No one else has what I have. I have had nine days to heal old wounds and open up my heart, open up my mother's heart. Nine days for a daughter, nine days for a mother, nine days to find my mother's love, nine days to learn to love my mother. I guess this is the true meaning of closure. The fact that we bonded during these days does not escape me; through tears, annoyance, patience, impatience, and alcohol for me, Genevieve and I became a united front in her decision to come home to die. I think this is what feeling at peace means.

I turn on the ignition, put the car in drive, and, with tears streaming down my face, head to the unfamiliar, unknown path leading me to my mother's death.

As I pull out of the hospital parking lot for the last time, I say out loud, "Let's get you home, Mom."

Three p.m.

"Hello?"

"Is this Sara Austin?"

"Yes, who's this?"

"Hello, Sara, this is Mary Armstrong from hospice, we spoke yesterday. I should be at your mother's house in about ten minutes."

"Mary, my mother isn't even there yet, I'm not there, nobody is there," I lie. Jess is there. I need to control whatever is happening. I have been in control for nine days, and I'm not about to let that go. So much for feeling at peace.

"Oh dear, when do you all expect to arrive?"

"I'm about thirty minutes away, and when I left my mother was still in her hospital bed waiting for the discharge papers to arrive."

"You say it takes you thirty minutes from the hospital to your mother's? I have Google-mapped it and even with traffic I would say no more than twenty at the most."

Oh, for god's sake, I think, this is not the time to nitpick with me, Hospice Lady.

"I need to make a few stops before I get there," I say to stall her.

"I have another client I need to see this afternoon. Let me see if I can change my schedule, which would bring me to your mother's closer to five o'clock. I'll let you know."

"Thanks so much." I hang up, not sure what I'm feeling right now. I have been in charge for the last nine days, in charge with Genevieve at my side, safe inside the hospital. I'm not sure I am fit to deal with 'the public.'

"I'm here," I yell as I try to open Genevieve's front door while carrying Jess's vase of dead flowers.

Jess comes running to the door to help. I haven't seen my sister in about two years, and it looks like she hasn't changed a bit. Jess and I look alike in some ways, but if you put us apart in a room of people you wouldn't guess that we are sisters. We are both about the same height, 5' 5", not fat, but not thin, and certainly could use some improvement in that category. I have shoulder-length blonde hair, a dark complexion, and green eyes. Jess is a brunette, hair cut short, and always perfect. She has porcelain skin and blue eyes. For the most part, I resemble Genevieve's side of the family, the Lemaires. At ninety-four, Genevieve wears her thick silver hair short, which shows off her startling green eyes and dark complexion. Parker and Ray look more like our father. They are both tall, about six feet, with dark brown hair, pale complexion, and blue eyes. Jess got the best of both sides. One thing that we all have in common is our smiles. When we smile together, our broad, toothy grins make it quite evident we are related.

"What are those awful things?" Jess asks, looking at the vase I'm holding.

"The flowers you sent Mom," I say as I kiss my sister on the cheek. "The house looks nice, it smells nice."

"I'll throw them out and show you what I've done." Jess takes the vase out of my hands, walks into the kitchen, and throws the vase, water, and flowers into the trash. Glad I drove them home.

The house does look nice, but it always does. Genevieve has a great eye for design and her taste in art and furnishings are a testament to her flair.

The house we grew up in, in Danbury, Connecticut, was not meant for kids. The entire antique four-bedroom home looked like something out of a *House Beautiful* magazine. In the living room, Genevieve had the walls covered in a Schumacher Cloud Toile wallpaper in soft silver. The sofa was a large London Chesterfield, the floor was covered with layered oriental rugs, and the side chairs and tables were equally opulent. This was not a place for feet on the furniture and sticky fingers. The fireplaced dining room was designed in a French countryside style, with two chandeliers placed perfectly above the trestle table for twelve. There was not a place in our childhood home for us to be actual kids. Even our bedrooms were perfect, decorated for each child to Genevieve's taste. She never asked for our input on what we would like our rooms to look like.

Jess brings me down the hall to Genevieve's master suite, her domain. It consists of a large master bath with a soaking tub and separate shower, a massive walk-in closet, a lovely reading nook with a down-filled loveseat, lots of books and decorating magazines, and the bedroom itself, with skylights, fireplace, and a chandelier.

In place of her queen-size bed is the hospital bed. Genevieve had balked at this quite strongly. She desperately needed to keep up appearances. With the persuasion of hospice, the doctor, and myself, she agreed, but was not happy. However, Jess has taken a generic hospital bed, one that screams "someone is dying here" and turned it into the best possible substitution. Genevieve's throw pillows are arranged and fluffed to perfection. Her luxurious comforter lies on top of hospital sheets, which are covered by Egyptian six-hundred-thread-count sheets, and her Company Store down blanket. The dreaded hospital tray is hidden under a tapestry cloth and discreetly placed in the corner of the room. A beautiful arrangement of flowers is on her bureau. A gift from one of her grandchildren.

"Wow, it looks great in here," I say as my phone rings. "Hello?"

"Hi, this is Jane Sullivan. I can't seem to find your house."

"Ummm, are you the hospice nurse?"

"No, I'm the harpist."

"Did you say harpist? Are you sure you're looking for us?"

"Yes, Genevieve Austin, that's who I'm looking for. I hope I'm not too late."

I look at my sister, shaking my head, and hand Jess my phone. Obviously, I cannot deal with the public.

"You talk to this person, I don't know who the fuck this is, why she's coming here, and why the fuck doesn't she have GPS?"

I am ready to explode. Where is the ambulance, where is Genevieve? Where is my mother?

In the background I can hear Jess. "Hi, this is Jessica Austin. And you are? Oh, from hospice, okay. Where are you exactly? Alright, sounds like you are a few miles away but headed in the right direction. Well, just stay on Route 53, and eventually you'll see black iron gates on your left. Turn there. What? Oh, sure, I can hang on until you find the gates."

I am glaring at my sister, who is sounding incredibly reasonable.

"Oh good, yes, drive through the gates. In about a mile or so, you'll see a row of mailboxes on your right. Go past those. Yes, I'll wait 'til you see them. Once you see the boxes you will go just a short distance—no, I'm not sure how many feet, not many though, and take your first left onto Lafayette Park. The house is on the right, number 6. You should be here soon. Call back if you can't find us."

While Jess hangs up from whoever that person was, Genevieve arrives home in the dreaded ambulance and is brought through her front door in a wheelchair. I know this is not how she wants it to be, but she is home, and her daughters are here for her. There was a long time when

Jess and I didn't speak, but here we are together for our mother.

I take a step back and let Jess welcome her home. Jess takes over. "Hi, Mom, I made you soup, how do you feel, you look wonderful, let me show you what I've done with your room."

I, on the other hand, am at the refrigerator looking for wine, which I am happy to say Jess has stocked with enough Chardonnay, Pinot Noir, and Rosé to—well, to be sure the family is well hydrated.

Genevieve gets a tour of her own place, loves the flowers, accepts the bed, and laughs at the creative disguise of the hospital tray.

Before leaving the hospital, Genevieve had received another dose of morphine for the ride home. She was dizzy and needed to lie down, as well as vomit. I could tell that Jess was out of her element—caretaker for her mother is not in her DNA. It's not in mine either, but I stepped in, not sure where the strength was coming from. I do not want any part of this. I don't want to be nurturing, if this is what nurturing is. Genevieve is my mother, not my child.

"Mom, let's get you on the couch. Jess, get a basin."

It's a struggle to get Genevieve comfortable, but somehow I manage. Jess brings the basin, and then the two of us just stand there watching as Genevieve tries to vomit. She hasn't eaten, so it's only bile. Genevieve relaxes against the pillows and immediately falls asleep.

The doorbell rings. "Damn, who is that?" I whisper, not wanting to wake up Genevieve.

Jess goes to the door and brings a woman with what looks like a large gun case into the living room.

"Sara, this is Jane, Jane is the harpist. Hospice sent Jane, and she has had a bit of difficulty trying to find the house. Jane, this is our mother, Genevieve. I'm sorry that she's sleeping right now." My sister sounds like she's reading a script from some comedy sketch.

The three of us turn and look at Genevieve, out cold from the morphine.

"Well, I am just glad I made it in time. So often I'm just a few minutes too late, the loved one has passed—then I just play for the family," Jane says.

Jess and I leave Jane to play her harp, which she removes from the large case, then starts to strum the most beautiful sound either of us has ever heard.

"This is so fucking bizarre, yet soothing at the same time," I say, more to myself than to Jess. "I wish she could play just a bit louder."

The soothing sounds from the living room are working their magic on my blood pressure, headache, and my general sense of exhaustion.

"She doesn't want to wake Mom. When is Parker arriving? And what about Ray?" Jess asks while opening a bottle of Chardonnay.

"I think tomorrow. What about Ray? You talked to him, right?"

"Yes, I talked to him, I told you I talked to him. I told him someone would keep him updated, but I haven't had a chance to do that with everything that's happening," Jess snaps while pouring the wine.

"Jesus, Jess, Ray should be here."

"I am sure he will be here; I just don't know when. Shit. Who's that in the driveway? Stash the wine."

Hospice has arrived. Jess and I feel like the cavalry is

here to save us.

Hospice Mary settles at the dining-room table, while Jane the harpist continues to play her beautiful music. She opens up a three-ring binder and begins to go over the extensive paperwork. What hospice does, other agencies to contact, important phone numbers, and more importantly what hospice doesn't do.

"No, we do not provide round-the-clock care. Your mother cannot be alone in the house. Someone needs to be home with her at all times. If you find yourself in a situation in which that isn't possible, we can arrange for an aide to come and stay, but for no more than two hours."

I am quite sure that I explained this to Jessica more than once, but the look on her face is one of shock.

"Let's move on to how to administer the morphine."

I find this part terrifying. What if we give her too much, not enough? What if we get it on our hands? Is this stuff even legal?

Hospice Mary is extremely thorough and incredibly kind, somewhat like a rudder to our tippy dingy. She shows us how to fill up the syringe and then watches as Jess and I each take a few turns to be sure we use the exact dosage prescribed. Next, she explains the need to follow Genevieve's wishes to die with dignity. "Your mother has determined that she does not want to continue living in her current condition. To help her with her wishes you should limit her food and fluid intake. There are a couple of reasons for this. One is that any food will exacerbate her bowel and digestive issues. The more food she takes in, the sooner the symptoms that she had when she was admitted to the hospital will return. This could lead to increased discomfort, pain, and a return to the hospital. Limiting fluids will help her on her journey. However, if your mother asks for food or something to drink, don't hold back. Offer her small portions and allow her to enjoy them. It's very typical for patients to ask for certain foods, turkey dinner, for example. I say indulge your mother. If she is typical, she'll eat only a bite or two."

Jane the harpist is packing up when Hospice Mary finally says her goodbyes, leaving us with enough morphine to kill something much larger than a hundred-and-nine-pound ninety-four-year-old woman. In other words, enough morphine for us to kill Genevieve.

"What the hell?" Jess says, pouring more wine. "How long can we do this? Someone, one of us, needs to be here all the time. How long is she going to live? I hope for a long time, but seriously, we need to get her twenty-four-hour care. I'm not sure she can afford that. I'm not sure we can afford that. I can't stay here forever; I can't do this alone."

"Nobody is asking you to stay, Jess. Let's just get through the next couple of days to figure things out." I need my sister to be strong, because I can't stay here forever either, and I can't do this alone.

"Hello?" Damn, it's Beth calling and it's way past five p.m.

"Hi, Sara, is this a good time to talk? I only have a few free minutes, but I did want to get back to you and discuss a few things. First, I got your list of tasks and the time spent on each, so thanks for getting that to me. Sara, do you feel that you are busy enough to warrant your salary? In other words, are your days full or do you have a lot of down time? From what you sent, I don't see this as being a full-time position."

Oh my god, are you kidding me? I close my eyes, try to

take a breath. "My position is never a black-and-white day. There are days where I can't keep up, and then there are days that are quieter, which gives me a chance to work on projects."

"Okay, I get that, but I guess I don't get why you're still working; don't you want to retire or something? What is it that you want, Sara?"

I want you to jump off a bridge, that's what I want. Beth, you are a walking HR nightmare. I chose to ignore the retirement question. "I want to be a part of this company; I want to be able to say that I contributed to its growth. I want to continue to be a part of this dynamic team."

"That all sounds good, but my understanding is that you need to step up. I had one partner tell me that he wouldn't trust anything that comes across his desk from you."

"Who said that?" I am losing my composure.

"Jeff Moriarty told me that. I had to ask around to get an idea of what others think of you and your job performance. And that's what Jeff said."

"Did anyone else have complaints about me?" I hate Jeff, even more so now.

"No, everyone else had good things to say."

So, you are focusing on the one bad review and basing your judgment of me on one person's opinion. *Fuck all of you.*

"Well, I'm not sure why Jeff would say that. He's difficult to work with and difficult to please. I do my best to accommodate him, but he's not the only person in this company that I do things for. Jeff can't always think that he's my number-one priority." My voice sounds calm, but

I am shaking with anger.

"Sara, I just want you to be aware of what he said. You need to be sure you double-check, triple-check your work. Maybe I'll talk to Brett about cutting back on your hours. Just something to think about. Bye."

I hang up the phone and just start crying. How much more can I take of this stupid job, especially while my mother is dying?

"Oh, Sara, that didn't sound good. What happened?"

Through tears, I tell Jess what Beth said: cutting down on my hours, retirement, stupid Jeff. I say that I don't understand why Beth would only focus on the negative, not the positive.

"She sounds like a woman trying to keep up with the men in this company, trying to make a name for herself. There's nothing wrong with that, I actually know that feeling. But unfortunately, she uses discouragement rather than encouragement. Your Beth sounds like a piece of work and she has lousy management skills. But that doesn't help you out with this current situation. I'd say you could report her to HR, but honestly, that would only make your life more miserable. You work for what is considered a fairly small company, it's not like you could work in a different department. Sara, have you told them about Mom?"

"No, I don't want them to use this against me."

"I don't think they can do that."

"Jess, it doesn't matter. I need this job and I just need to pull myself together. Where's the wine?" In true Austin tradition, we drink rather than face our fears. While I blow my nose and wait for the wine, I wonder, what do I want? World peace, a mansion on the ocean? But in my heart, my soul, what do I want? The sad answer is I don't know what I want. I am such a reactionary person, act then think. I can't say oh, I wish I had gone to veterinary school and now had my own successful clinic. Looking back at what I wish I had done, doesn't help with what I wish or want what I have now. I do know that I need to look ahead, not back. I regret that I hadn't planned better to feel secure in my future. I regret that I hate this job now. I regret that I let my family dynamics shape who I am today. I can't let this life be about regrets, I have so much to be thankful for. I think it's time for Sara Austin to learn to love herself, as is, and get on with her life.

Genevieve wakes up—all hands on deck. She's hungry and wants a glass of wine. Jess and I are thrilled. This is just a bump in the Genevieve road; everything will be better tomorrow. I sit on the couch with my sister and my mother and think, here we are, the three Austin women sitting together sipping wine, eating cheese and crackers. Well, one Austin woman is sipping her wine—Jess and I are slugging ours and devouring the cheese and crackers. This could seem almost normal if you were on the outside looking in.

"I need to go to the bathroom right now," Genevieve says, handing me her wine glass.

Jess grabs the walker and I jump into action and the two of us try to lift Genevieve off the couch. None of this is a pretty picture. She is dead weight—poor choice of words—but we do get Genevieve to the bathroom. It's horrible, but I get her to the toilet just a second too late. Well, at least she isn't constipated anymore, I think, as I tell her to move her feet so she doesn't step in anything. Genevieve is in a morphine-wine haze and I can see that she is trying desperately to maintain her dignity as I help her not step in her own poop. The only reason I know how to deal with this is that I watched a nurse doing the same thing in the hospital with her. Don't put your foot there, Genevieve, try to move over. How in the world am I doing this? But I clean it up and watch Genevieve Austin accept that things are never going to be the same for her again. This is degrading, this is awful, this is what she—what we—are facing? God, why couldn't you make death easier? Meanwhile, Jess is standing outside of the bathroom looking horrified. I can relate. Welcome home, sis.

Jess and I get Genevieve into the hospital bed as if nothing has happened. We Austins are really good at that, pretending everything is great. It's ten p.m. and Genevieve says, "Let's have more wine." I am on it, more wine for all.

As I leave to get the wine, I glance back and hear Genevieve say to her oldest child, "Jessica, are you okay with this, all of this, what I have decided? Ultimately it is my decision, but I would like to know that I can go in peace. I want you to understand why I have chosen to not fight this time. I am done fighting, Jessica."

I can hear my sister trying to sound strong. "I wish this wasn't happening, but, yes, I am okay with your decision. I will do whatever you need me to do."

"I need you to understand that I don't want to live like this. I told Sara; she knows what to do. Jessica, I am not afraid to die."

I leave my mother and sister alone, and then quietly return to the bedroom with the wine. Genevieve is asleep, and Jess is crying.

The morphine schedule is midnight, three a.m., six a.m., and so on, every three hours. Jess and I stay up together drinking wine, bonding, and bitching until midnight, and do that 'feeding' together. It's hard. Genevieve isn't quite awake, but we can both sense that she is aware of something.

Jess offers to take the three a. m. shift since I've been on for the last nine days. I'm not sure why, but I decide to sleep on the couch in the living room, right outside Genevieve's room. Jess takes one of the upstairs guest rooms. I'm restless but exhausted. I need to sleep. As I finally start to doze off, I hear my sister in the upstairs bathroom vomiting. What the hell, I think, sitting up. Jess yell-whispers, "Sorry, it's food poisoning."

"Well, since we didn't eat, I rule out food poisoning."

Jess continues to vomit, and I do the three a.m. alone. "It's okay, Mom," I say as I measure out the exact dose of morphine instructed by Hospice Mary. "It's okay, Mom," I say as I pull her cheek out and dispense the liquid. "It's okay, Mom." I sit in my mother's room listening to her breathing and close my eyes, wondering what the hell I am doing. Is this really okay, Mom?

SIBLINGS MINUS ONE

"The family. We were a strange little band of
characters trudging through life."
— Erma Bombeck

I do Genevieve's six a.m. morphine 'feeding,' letting Jess sleep.

Once Jess is up and showered, she spends most of the morning explaining to me why she vomited for the majority of last night. I get it, Jessica is so stressed, and this is how her body chooses to deal with it. Wonder what my body is choosing to do?

Genevieve is awake, a bit groggy, but lets us know that's she's hungry and wants breakfast, preferably a soft-boiled egg, with toast and tea. We don't know what to do. The plan is to not feed our mother. If she eats, she prolongs the inevitable, but by prolonging that, the chance of the fluids and the pain returning is guaranteed. Jess and I are trying not to panic. What the hell are we supposed to do?

Jess gives Genevieve a sip of water and she quickly seems to forget that she said she was hungry and dozes off. I'm not sure if this is a good thing, but to be honest, I'm not sure of anything right now.

It has been prearranged by hospice that a hospice team

member would come in at nine a.m. every morning, seven days a week. And right on time, the doorbell rings. Jess opens the door and welcomes a lovely older woman, past middle age, gray hair, scrubs with a Winnie-the-Pooh design on the top, and clogs. Jess brings her into Genevieve's room. "Mom, this is Beverly, Beverly, this is Genevieve."

Genevieve smiles and puts out her hand. "Hello, Beverly, who are you?" Beverly explains to Genevieve who she is and why she's there. "Genevieve, I'm here to check your vitals and get you up to the bathroom and help you bathe, help you to feel comfortable."

"Oh dear, I suppose I do need help." Genevieve sounds to me like she has accepted what she needs to do to get through whatever time she has left and try to maintain as much dignity as possible.

Jess and I leave Mom with Beverly and walk into the kitchen together.

"You know that I couldn't do what Beverly does," Jessica says, almost to herself, as she drinks another large glass of water.

"Me neither. I don't have a nursing bone in my body." But right now, I need to log in and work. I need to work and give my mother morphine every three hours. How crazy is this?

The doorbell rings again; it's Hospice Mary.

"Good morning, Mary," Jess says, bringing Mary into the kitchen. "Beverly is in with Genevieve."

"How was your night?" Mary asks.

"Well, I had food poisoning," Jess offers.

"Jess, I think Mary is asking how our night with Genevieve was, something that you have no idea of." I guess that was a bit snarky, but damn it, I am exhausted.

Jess just glares at me, probably grateful that Beverly has come into the room.

"Genevieve is back in her bed. I changed it so she has fresh sheets and new blankets. I think she feels better in a clean nightgown and a fresh bed. We did have some difficulty with a bowel movement. I am afraid that she's close to being blocked again. She is resting now." Beverly packs up her bag. "I will see you both tomorrow morning."

Hospice Mary has brought more morphine with her and goes over again how to be sure we are providing the right dosage. "I am concerned that Beverly mentioned your mother's bowel movement issue this morning. Let me go in and visit with her a bit if that is okay with both of you."

"Yes, of course," Jess and I say in unison.

"Are you hungry, Jess? I'm starving," I say, looking in the fridge. There is nothing in there but one quart of chicken soup, wine, and some condiments.

"God, no, I could still throw up," she says, getting up from the table, away from me, the morphine, and the display of illness, and going into the living room.

"Okay, well, I guess I'll refrigerate the morphine, Jess. I hope nobody gets thirsty and decides this would be something to drink." I hope Hospice Mary didn't hear me. I need a break from this, but there is no way I am letting up—this is my job now. Speaking of job, damn, I still need to log into work.

Hospice Mary has Genevieve up and together they are trying to make the short walk from bed to the living-room couch. Genevieve is very weak and unsteady, but is determined to not spend the day in bed. Once Genevieve is settled on the couch, pillows propped, covered in a soft sheet and a cashmere blanket, Mary quietly asks to speak to us in the kitchen and updates us on Genevieve's condition.

"I gave your mother a suppository, which should help her to feel more comfortable for the moment. However, she's going to need another in a few hours."

One look at my sister tells me Jess wants to vomit again. I want no part of this suppository situation either.

"After spending this time with Genevieve, I feel that her condition is deteriorating faster than anticipated."

"How so? I mean, what does this mean, what are you saying?" Jess asks.

"From my years of experience in this field, working with numerous people in hospice and evaluating your mother's recent symptoms, I would think five or six days, maybe a week at best. I'm sorry."

"Hello, hello," from the front door.

Jess, Hospice Mary, and I all turn to look at Parker and Jill arriving with bags of groceries.

"Hi, everyone, we're here, finally. We got in late last night after eight hours of traveling, we are tired, but we're here. We left Brady sleeping at home. Parker and I figured that was best until we knew what we are facing," Jill says, kissing Jess and then me on the cheek.

Meanwhile, Jess and I are trying to process what Hospice Mary just said. Maybe a week, if we are lucky? What happened to two to three months?

Parker went straight into the living room, to the couch. "Look at you, Mom. You look great."

"Oh, do I?" Genevieve asks, perking up for her son, making a lame attempt at fluffing her hair.

"How are you feeling?"

"Well, I have been better," she chuckles. "I am so hungry."

That was a red flag for Jess and me. We look at each other, eyes wide, no words needed between us. Jessica and I are on the same wavelength.

"Okay, well, I made you chicken soup," he says, holding up one of the bags he brought in. When the hell did he have time to make homemade chicken soup? "Do you want me to heat that up for you?"

"That would be so nice, Parker, thank you."

Jill sits next to her mother-in-law. "Genevieve, how are you feeling? What happened? You were so good at Christmas." Jill is genuinely concerned, but I know that she is probably thinking, now that she and Parker are home, they can take over, things will improve.

Parker gets busy in the kitchen, putting away groceries, pulling out a pan to heat up the soup. Jess walks by our brother and says, "I made homemade chicken soup too, you know."

"Great, plenty of soup for all." Our brother isn't going to fall into their old competitive ways.

I'm struggling to hold in my temper, indignation. I'm the one who's been taking care of Genevieve for more than nine days. I know what she needs and doesn't need. And what she does not need is fucking chicken soup. Typical Parker to think that I can't handle this—well, screw you, Parker Austin.

"Parker," Jill calls from the living room, "can you come here, please?"

While the chicken soup is heating up, Genevieve tells Parker and Jill that what she would really like is some real Cream of Wheat with brown sugar and butter. "Nothing like that stuff they tried to pass off as Cream of Wheat in the hospital."

"Sure," says Parker, getting up to turn off the chicken soup that he had made from scratch with horrific jet lag.

As Parker puts on his coat he says, "I'm going to get Cream of Wheat," to anyone listening.

I'm listening. I follow my brother out the front door.

"What do you think you're doing, Parker?"

"I told you; I'm going to get Mom her Cream of Wheat."

"Look, Parker, I know that you haven't been completely filled in on Mom's wishes, but Cream of Wheat is not part of the plan."

"What are you talking about, Sara? Mom wants Cream of Wheat, and I am going to get it for her."

"Fuck the Cream of Wheat, Parker, she isn't supposed to be eating."

"Sara, calm down, obviously you're exhausted, and your language is deplorable. Go home, I'm here now. I'll take over, you should rest. You look awful." I hate this side of Parker, Mr. Condescending.

"I am not going anywhere, Parker; I have been here since day one. I am the one who has been dealing with Mom and I am going to see this to the end. Which, by the way, you'll just prolong by feeding her."

"What are you talking about? You aren't making sense, Sara."

"Come back in the house and I'll fill you in."

I know that Parker is not going along with crazy Sara and whatever her "fill you in" means, but he follows me back into the house. He goes back to the living room and sits down in a chair across from Genevieve. Parker's tanned vacation complexion has turned to an ashen color. He looks exhausted too. While he and I were outside discussing the pros and cons of Cream of Wheat, Jess gave Genevieve her twelve-o'clock morphine feeding. I'm pretty sure that Jill didn't know what to make of this as she witnessed the dosing and watched her mother-in-law slip into a morphine stupor and fall asleep sitting up on the couch.

Hospice Mary is still in the kitchen. "Parker, come sit with us," Jess calls. I watch as my brother slowly gets up and walks into the kitchen. He looks old, I think as I follow him in.

"Mary, this is our brother Parker. Parker, this is Mary from hospice. She has been helping us with Genevieve." Hospice Mary and Parker shake hands politely. "Parker, why don't you sit down?" Jess asks. He does and listens to Jess explain what Genevieve's end-of-life wishes are.

"This is nuts. She's my mother, too. Sara has just filled her head with this crazy crap. You're giving her morphine to kill her. You have got to be kidding me. I'm sure there are other options, other choices here. What about bringing her to Boston, a specialist? Anybody think of that? Has anybody thought of anything other than this crazy plan? This has Sara written all over it." Parker is struggling to maintain control.

Jess gives me a look to keep quiet. She gets up and walks over to look out the front window. Jessica takes just a minute before she turns to look her brother straight in the eye. "Parker, Mom has advanced stomach cancer, no specialist in the world can cure that. Mom was in a lot of pain. Parker, she wanted to die even before she got the diagnosis. This is Mom's decision, no one else's. Case closed."

I watch my brother take a breath, center himself. With a quiet, calm demeanor, he turns to Hospice Mary. "Why do you feel the need to give my mother this drug, why morphine? There has to be another way. Why can't she have Cream of Wheat if she wants it? Why can't she have anything she wants if all of you think that she is just going to die anyway?"

Mary goes on to explain to Parker Genevieve's condition and her prognosis. Jill is standing just outside the kitchen.

"But why give her a narcotic that she'll get addicted to?"

Hospice Mary is a saint, I think, listening to her patiently explain the reasons for the morphine.

"Your mother is receiving the morphine to alleviate the pain that she has been in, to keep her calm, to help with a feeling of overall peace, to help her enjoy her last days. There isn't enough time left for your mother to become addicted to morphine. I am so sorry," she says, softly.

"Okay, I'll try to process all of this, but why is Sara saying she can't eat?"

Hospice Mary explains that because Genevieve's body is shutting down, feeding her will only cause pain and discomfort because her body can no longer digest and expel waste due to the cancer in her stomach. "Your mother isn't being denied food or liquid. If she wants to eat something, of course, she should have it. But as you saw with the chicken soup, your mother's hunger doesn't last long, and then she forgets about it. She basically no longer feels hungry. We suggest you offer liquids to help keep her lips moist. Sometimes a wet cloth held gently to her mouth will offer a bit of comfort."

"Sara said she has a few months to live. We can't keep denying her food and doping her up for that long. How long do you think my mother really has left to live?" I can hear the struggle in his voice; those are hard words to say.

"I can't predict it exactly, but your mother's bowel symptoms are returning, much sooner than expected, which means her pain is increasing. I would say that she might have five or six days, not much longer than that."

Jill stands behind her husband, rubbing his shoulders. "Mary, could you please show us how to administer the morphine? We need to help out with this. Parker, honey, this is what Genevieve wants. You and I need to pitch in here, and we need to do it the right way."

Jess and I watch as Parker and Jill practice filling syringes with morphine. Hospice Mary leaves only when she is sure that they can administer it correctly.

The house is silent. None of us says a word. Parker looks around at Jess, at me, at his dying mother, and at his wife, who is his rock. My heart is breaking for him. Since Genevieve was admitted to the hospital two weeks ago, Jess and I have been talking, putting things in order. We didn't include Parker, just told him when to come home. I would imagine in his mind he had no idea that he would be coming home to chaos, insanity, hospice, a dying mother who is getting morphine, thanks to me. I'm sure he is thinking what the hell has happened to his world.

Well, no time for feeling sorry for Parker, no time to feel sorry for anyone. We have less time than we thought. We have stuff to do.

"Someone needs to call Ray. I'll call Liza, Emma, and the cousins. Jess, can you call the Ms and Kathy? I think that we are going to have to tell people when they can come. The top priority should be our kids and Emma. Jess, when do you think Russ, Julie, and Andrew can be here? I think we are going to be okay for the next week, right, you guys?" God, I hope we have more time than that. I am really worried.

"Parker, you call Ray," Jess orders. Jill starts opening wine.

The calls have been made and we are sitting at Genevieve's kitchen table, drinking wine, trying to figure out what to order in for a late lunch or maybe an early dinner, who knows at this point? Nobody wants to eat the two quarts of homemade chicken soup sitting in the refrigerator. Parker is waiting to do the six p.m. doping and then he and Jill are going home. They'll be back tomorrow for the long haul with their son Brady.

"Liza is coming tomorrow after Max gets out of school. Tess is coming on Sunday. Emma will be coming around noon. I think that we can hold off on the cousins until Monday," I say, sipping my wine, fighting off the exhaustion that is setting in. I had called Keith, let him know the latest on Genevieve, and told him I wouldn't be home tonight, maybe tomorrow, but definitely not tonight.

"I'll be there tomorrow. Give Genevieve a kiss for me and call me if you need anything before I head over. Try to get some sleep, baby," he said before hanging up.

"I told May and Maureen that they can come to visit Sunday afternoon. I just asked that they call first to make sure Mom is up for it, I am sure she will be, the same for Kathy. I think my side of the family is in good shape. Julie and Andrew are looking into flights, maybe a redeye Saturday, which will get them here around noon on Sunday. Russ is going to try to get out first thing tomorrow morning. Where the hell is everyone going to stay? Parker, what about Ray?" Jess asks.

"He didn't answer."

We all seem to ignore or choose to not pay attention to the fact that Hospice Mary had told the family to be prepared for their mother not making it more than five or six days.

It's time for Parker to give Genevieve her morphine. He lets us help him, to make sure he's giving her the drug the right way. "If I'm going to do this, then I am going to do it right," he says, squirting the poison under his mother's cheek. "This isn't what I want to do, Mom," Parker whispers in her ear. *We know, Parker, your sisters know.*

He and Jill leave shortly after. Jess and I will handle the rest of the dosages for one more night.

I get into a pair of Genevieve's pajamas; I haven't packed right. I didn't think I would still be here. What did I think? I am exhausted, both from lack of sleep and also from keeping my feelings and emotions at bay. My mother is dying but I need to put that on the back burner, simmering for now.

"Go to bed," Jess says after we do the midnight dosage together. "I'll sleep on the couch outside of Mom's room, that loveseat is too small to stretch out on. You go upstairs, sleep. I promise to do both the three and six a.m. feedings."

"I will take you up on that. Goodnight, Jess," I say, bringing my wine upstairs and falling into the guest-room queen-size bed.

Jess gets settled in on the couch and falls right to sleep. From the sounds of the snoring below, it sounds like a dead sleep—poor choice of words, again.

I can't sleep, my heart is racing, I must be overtired or something. Shit, I haven't been taking any of my evening meds. How long have I been here, how many nights have I missed? How bad is it to skip thyroid, high blood pressure, and anti-depression prescriptions? Great, let's just add withdrawal to my life achievements. So now that I am aware of what I'm not taking and what I should be taking, I become more anxious. I cannot calm down. I give up, turn on the light, and think about what Genevieve had said about the guest-room closet being a mess. I get out of bed, in Genevieve's beautiful silk pajamas, and open the closet door. It's two a.m.—this is insane. Whatever, I can't sleep.

The closet is a large walk-in and, yes, Genevieve does have a massive pile, actually piles, of papers from Morgan Stanley, paper copies of her investments. Jess had mentioned that she has been trying for years to get Genevieve to stop getting paper copies, she could just see them online, but Genevieve insisted on getting the paper copies so she could go over each one, line by line. But I am more interested in the clothes hanging in the closet. These are dresses from my mother's past, bright, colorful caftans, rhinestone dresses from the disco era, miniskirts, maxi skirts, formal gowns, and then, there it is—my wedding dress. Genevieve had tried to give it back to me, but I didn't have a place for it, so it languished in the guest-room closet with the piles of papers.

This is the dress I married Keith in. Wonder if it still fits, twenty-something years later? Oh, what the hell. Off come my mother's pajamas and I slip the beautiful, beaded dress off its hanger. Damn, it's heavy, I think, gingerly stepping into it and pulling it up over my thighs, hips, belly, past my sports bra, and there it is sitting on my shoulders. Can I still fit in it; do I dare zip it up? I struggle to pull the zipper up. Seriously, it was snug then—the actual description is fitted, I think, trying to zip up a bit more. I stop. What if I get stuck in this dress, what if I can't unzip it? Would I have to have the rescue squad come, sirens blaring, and use the Jaws of Life to free me? That would be beyond embarrassing. I step out of my dress and hang it back in the closet. As I'm getting back into Genevieve's pajamas, I notice it's three a.m., with no noise from downstairs.

Jess is out cold on the couch. She is a good sleeper and I hate her for that, I think as I walk past her. It's three in the morning, the house is dark except for the light in the kitchen, and I am alone at the kitchen table, bottle of morphine and syringe in my hands. Am I murdering my mother? I hesitate for only an instant, walk past my sleeping sister, into Genevieve's room, administer the morphine as directed. "Oh Mom, oh Mom, I'm so sorry this is happening to you," I whisper into her ear. Genevieve raises her hand, just a bit, her eyes slightly open. "Don't be sad, Sara, if I know that you kids are okay, then I'm okay."

I lie down next to my mother in her hospital bed, fighting back tears, "We're okay. Mom. We are okay."

"Promise me, Sara."

"I promise, Mom." My mother closes her eyes, and we lie silently together. No sound other than her breathing. I don't dare move, afraid to disturb her.

"Sara, are you still here?"

"Yes, Mom, I'm right here, right next to you."

"I'm drifting away, I'm drifting in a sailboat. There's no breeze, it's calm, Sara, it's calm and you kids are okay. It's so very calm." Genevieve falls into a deep sleep.

A REPRIEVE OF TOGETHERNESS

"The trouble is you think you have time."
– Gautama Buddha

"**G**ood morning, Nurse Jackie," I say to Jess as I finish Genevieve's six a.m. dosage.

"Oh, I am so sorry. I told you I'm a deep sleeper, but I can do the six o'clock. I told you I would do it."

"It's past six, Jess, I did the three and the six, you missed both."

"Oh damn, really, you did both?"

"Yup, maybe you can make me some coffee," I say, smiling at my sister. In the grand scheme of things, this isn't the end of the world. That was coming, but Jess sleeping through her shifts, not a big deal. And there it is, another slight shift in Sara Austin, I think as I get up and try to clear my exhausted brain.

Jess and I sit in the kitchen sipping our coffee. "How was Mom last night?" Jess asks.

"She woke up a little bit, just for a minute, but that means she's still with us. I guess what I mean is that she's still conscious. We still have time." I'm keeping my conversation with Genevieve to myself. I sip my coffee, look out the window. It's another gray February day. "She would hate this weather, you know."

"Yes, she would hate it. I hate it, it's depressing. By the way, I'm going to have to go to a local Morgan Stanley office this morning. I've been working with Genevieve's investors, getting her finances organized so we don't have to go through probate. Mom doesn't want to have her money tied up after she's gone." Jessica sighs and shakes her head. "This is all so exhausting," she says.

"It is exhausting, but we can't stop now. We need to be here for Mom, or at least I do."

"Don't be like that, Sara, I'm sorry I slept through the night, you should have woken me up."

"That's not what I meant; I don't know why I said that. I'm going to go take a shower and then I have two conference calls this morning, so I'll work out of the guest room."

I feel old, I think as I go up the stairs, old and tired. It seems so unfair. My mother dying downstairs and I'm calling into work, pretending the whole world revolves around this company.

I can see Jess downstairs doing her own work at the dining-room table. As Genevieve's executrix, she's been working behind the scenes, determined to get Genevieve's affairs in order as soon as possible. Jess already has signing privileges on all of Genevieve's accounts, but her extensive research has shown that when Genevieve passes, Jess loses those rights. She's been scrambling with Genevieve's investor group to move as quickly as possible to give Jess all financial authority. This has been a herculean effort for her, but she isn't one to shy away from a challenge.

Jessica turns on her laptop and starts transferring

funds from Genevieve's account to her own. She already told me we're going to need cash on hand for all the little expenses down the road—basically, a lot of wine. She's also made sure that she pays all of Genevieve's bills. I know that Jessica feels bad, not just about oversleeping, but about everything. Jess has told me more than once that she feels like she has let me down over these two weeks. I told her that was crazy and that I didn't feel that way at all. And to be truthful, I don't feel that way.

"But Sara, you had to deal with some intense medical conversations with both doctors and Mom. I'm not sure I could do what you have done."

"Well, I sure couldn't do what you're doing with all the financial stuff. You're doing more than just following Mom's wishes. You're making sure that the four of us are taken care of, no probate, no attorneys. That is a huge load off my mind. So, thank you."

Jess had already made sure Genevieve's will was up to date, signed by two witnesses, and notarized. The will was straightforward: everything was to be divided equally among the four of us. It was Jess who discovered that we needed a Living Trust to avoid probate. Jess made sure that our mother had a Healthcare Proxy she felt comfortable with, someone who would carry out her wishes, but also would be strong enough to offer choices. That of course was me. She made sure that I had it signed, witnessed, and notarized. Jess is the one that sent notices to all of Genevieve's numerous health providers, including the Do Not Resuscitate Order, and fought with our mother until Genevieve agreed to put it on her refrigerator so emergency responders would see it.

I hear Beverly arrive right on time, say good morning

to Jess, and head straight to Genevieve's room.

I close the bathroom door and turn the shower as hot as I can handle. It feels good, but I can't linger here. Time to get back to life, to try to forget my mother is dying downstairs. I get dressed and dial in for my calls.

"Hi, everyone, Sara here."

My calls are shorter than usual. Very few participants had anything to update the team with, including stupid Jeff Moriarty. I am done with calls by eleven a.m.

"Okay, calls are done, hopefully, work is done for the day. I would like it if every workday was a two-hour day. I can't believe I am working while all of this is happening," I say, walking down the stairs. I feel lighter, more positive; today is going to be a good day. "Are you going to the Morgan Stanley office? I can stay with Mom."

"I think we should wait; Hospice Mary is with Mom." The fact that Hospice Mary is with Genevieve isn't unusual, but the way my sister looks when she says it sets off an alarm in my head.

"Is everything okay, has something changed?" I start to go into Genevieve's room. "I need to be with Mom."

"I don't actually know what's happening, other than Beverly suggested I call hospice and have them come here this morning. Why don't we wait for Mary to come out? Let's have another cup of coffee and I'll fill you in."

Jess pours us some coffee and begins to tell me what has transpired in the last two hours while I was upstairs working.

"Beverly arrived at her usual time. I could hear her talking to Genevieve, in a soft, soothing voice, telling her about her kids, her life, as if they were sitting down to tea. What a kind woman, I thought. I don't know how people like Beverly, Hospice Mary, and Jane the Harpist do what they do. And I don't know what we would do without them." Jess goes on, "I was still working on my PC trying to decipher the value of Mom's investments when Beverly asked if she could have a moment with me. She said, 'I think it would be prudent for you to call in your hospice worker.' I told her that hospice usually just stops in, we don't call. Beverly, as nice as can be, said, 'I suggest you do call. I can't give any comment or opinion on a patient, your mother, so it would be best if hospice is called.' Sara, I was so close to a panic attack, but I told Beverly that I'd call right then, and that's what I did. I don't think she was out the front door before I was on the phone."

"And then what?" I am dumbfounded listening to Jess; how could all of this have been happening one floor below me while I was on stupid conference calls?

"Well, I tried to get myself together. I took a few minutes and sat looking out the window, thinking how depressing this weather is. Anyway, I calmed down and went to check on Mom. I know that she's been in and out of consciousness, but I also know, regardless of her state, that I needed to act as if she heard every word I was saying."

"So, what happened?" I am still sitting in a stupefied state.

"I just sat with her, and quietly let her know that I was there for her. Sara, she knew I was there. I held her hand, I was trying so hard not to cry, I didn't want her to know that I was upset."

Of course, why would any of us let our dying mother know that this was upsetting? I keep that thought to myself.

"But then, she tried to open her eyes. It was awful, only

one would open. I said, 'I'm here Mom, I hope you know I'm here.' 'I know, Jess. I know you are here, dear. Stay, Jess.' That's what Mom said."

And then my sister starts sobbing.

"I said to her, 'I will, Mom, I promise, I will stay.' I told her that she made me strong and thanked her for that. And then I said, 'I love you.' Sara, I don't think I ever told her I loved her. I'm not sure if I ever really did love her—did she ever really love me? But at that moment I think I felt what it means to love your mother."

I reach across the table and touch my sister's hand. It's hard for us to show emotion, other than anger, but I feel such empathy for her private time with Genevieve and I'm grateful that she had that moment with our mother.

"Oh, Sara, this is so hard."

"Did Mom say anything else to you?"

Jess dries her eyes with a dishtowel hanging off the stove, not a Jess move at all. "She didn't sound as coherent after that. She mumbled something about a sailboat, the water, something about calm. It was hard to understand her. I don't know what she meant. Hospice Mary came in then and that's what happened in a short span of a couple of hours. More coffee?"

I'm in a state of disbelief; how could this be happening? I was only upstairs, just feet away from my mother. I feel like I'm losing control.

I take the hot mug of coffee Jess hands me, and out of nowhere she says, "I wish we could get the harpoonist back."

I look at her, baffled—what is she saying?—and then we both burst out laughing. "You mean the harpist, you idiot."

It was funny—not that funny, but it was obvious that

we needed a good laugh, and we probably needed the "harpoonist" as well.

"Shhh, I don't want Hospice Mary hearing us laughing." Jess and I smile at each other, two sisters facing the inevitable together.

"Thank goodness we have each other," I say to Jess.

"Yup, thank goodness for that. We are going to get through this, Sara, we are all going to be okay."

"We have to be," I say, "I promised Mom we would all be okay."

Hospice Mary quietly comes out of Genevieve's room and joins us in the kitchen.

Jess gets up. "Is everything okay? Well, I mean as okay as anything could be at this point."

Mary is putting papers into her briefcase. She seems different; I can sense that things aren't good. "I would like to update you both on your mother's condition. Beverly had alerted me to a decrease in activity with your mother. Beverly noticed that she is moving less, and she didn't respond to any questions this morning. Has she shown any interest in food or fluids in the last eight hours?"

Jess shoots me a look of *don't you dare tell her I slept through everything.* "I put some ice chips on her lips because they seemed really dry—she moved her lips, tried to lick them, I thought that meant she wanted a little bit of something cool on her lips. But no, she hasn't asked for any food or water in the last eight hours."

Now I want to vomit.

"Your mother's blood pressure has lowered significantly since yesterday, which is going to result in decreased blood flow to her hands and feet. Her body temperature is going down, just a bit, but these are all signs of your mother entering further into the dying process. To be quite honest, I've seen a significant change in your mother's condition just since yesterday."

"I'm sorry, Mary, for being so blunt, but what is it you're trying to tell us?" Jess asks in a very composed voice.

"I feel that your mother's decline is indicative of this process moving much quicker than anticipated. I would suggest you and your family be prepared to say your goodbyes this weekend. I know this is extremely difficult. No one is prepared for this, to say goodbye to a loved one. Please remember that there are going to be times she might be fully awake, and other times your mother might be completely unresponsive, or she may lapse into a coma. Even if she's in a coma, she may still be able to hear, understand, and recognize you. Hearing is one of the last senses to go before death. Please caution anyone who visits her to remember this. You don't want your mother to be agitated in any way. I would like to take just a few more minutes of your time to go over what's next."

For the next thirty minutes, we listen as Mary goes over what to do after your loved one passes, or something like that. She explains that we must call hospice as soon as Genevieve has passed. After that wait for about an hour and then call the crematorium, who will come to take her away. "They are very professional, sensitive to the situation," she says, as if that helps. Hospice Mary had already gone over the cost savings for a cremation done through a crematorium rather than through a funeral home. I don't think Genevieve would care one way or another. She wanted to be cremated, and I'm sure she would approve of us saving a couple of thousand dollars here. After all, at that point, I figure Genevieve will be long gone, off to other adventures.

"Once your mother has left you should call the furniture rental company for them to come and get the bed, table, and whatever else you rented. If you need me to come back later today, or tonight, you have my number. And all of this information is in the binder here, so don't worry if you forget anything. Please don't hesitate for even a second to call me."

Jess walks Hospice Mary to the front door.

It is just a little past noon. I wearily get out of my chair, take down two of my mother's wine glasses from her wine cabinet, and open up a bottle of Chardonnay. "Is it too early?" I ask as Jess comes back into the kitchen. As if that ever stopped any of us, I think.

"Of course not, we can just hide it when people come over. Oh, and it's time for Mom's noon doping. I'll do it, but I do need to talk to you about Mom's finances." And so, we move forward, move on, just as our mother would expect.

I watch Jess expertly fill the syringe with the morphine and walk to our mother's room. I can hear how she's trying to sound like life is normal as ever, especially since Hospice Mary reiterated that she might be able to hear us all the time. "Hi, Mom, it's me, Jess, time for your medicine." No response from Genevieve as Jess squirts the drug into the side of her mouth. Jess stands by the bedside trying to let the words "say your goodbyes" sink in. "I don't think I can ever say goodbye to you," my sister says as she walks out of the room.

Jess and I clink our wine glasses together and give a silent toast to our mother. Neither one of us is prepared for her to leave this quickly.

"This is starting to feel real," Jess says. "I need to call my kids and Russ. I don't know what to tell them. I don't want them coming here if she's in a coma, and Genevieve wouldn't want that. God, I don't know what to do." Jessica rarely feels defeated, but right at this moment, I know that she is.

I call Liza with the unpleasant update, as well as Parker and Ray. No one answers my call, so I leave messages. What has this world come to when you leave a message saying, "Hi, Genevieve is going to die much sooner than expected. You should probably try to get here ASAP." Whatever, I think as I drink my wine.

Emma arrives, unexpectedly. Emma, like her sister, does not use her cell phone. She has one, but it's just a nuisance. I stall Emma in the foyer while Jess removes all evidence of wine.

"Yes, well, this is quite a shock. We all thought that she had much more time, maybe they're wrong, nobody can predict this type of thing. She was supposed to have a stroke. Only God knows what the plan is."

"Well, I am sure that Genevieve will have a say in God's plan," I say, trying to lighten the mood up.

"You may be right, dear. Knowing my sister, she will probably have more than just a say." Emma looks like she is in shock herself. Less than two weeks ago, her sister was doing fine, not great, but after all, she is ninety-four years old. "Okay if I go sit with her?"

Parker and Jill arrive, quieter this time. The only food they bring is "to feed the troops," as Parker puts it. Keith arrives five minutes behind them. I am so grateful to have him here. I need a rock of my own. Jess and I quietly fill them in on the changes in Genevieve and what we should expect over the next couple of days.

Emma says her goodbyes. "I will make a novena for Genevieve tonight, at five o'clock service, and be back tomorrow."

"I'll open some wine." Jill knows her in-laws well.

"Hi, it's us," says Liza as she comes in the front door. "Surprise, look who I brought."

"I'm the surprise," says a smiling, nervous Ray.

Jess is the first to move. "Hello. Oh, Liza, so good to see you." She kisses Liza on the cheek and looks at her youngest brother. "Ray, hi, what a surprise."

I see that Jess is practically gritting her teeth, probably thinking, why the hell didn't you tell us, or why didn't Liza? But she keeps smiling, ushering everyone into the house. She gives Ray an awkward hug. I know that she is wondering where the hell he is going to sleep.

I hug Liza, whispering, "Where did you find Ray?"

"He texted me yesterday and said he was coming home. He didn't know who to call or what to do. I picked him up at the bus station. Mom, what was I supposed to do?"

"It's fine, Liza, you did the right thing. I kind of like that you're Uncle Ray's favorite," I say sarcastically.

"Damn, Mom, you look awful, what are you wearing?"

Liza is right. I do look awful, and to add to my run-down haggard look, I'm wearing Genevieve's clothes—a pink cowl-neck cashmere sweater with black velvet lounge pants.

"I'm wearing your grandmother's clothes. You don't approve?"

"Wow, that's cool that you can fit into her stuff, I

guess." Liza is laughing, reminding me why I adore her.

Parker and Jill get up to greet Liza and Ray.

Parker shakes his brother's hand and gives him a pat on the back. "Hey, man, how are you? It's good to see you. I wish the circumstances were different."

Jill, who always makes everyone she meets feel comfortable, says, "Hi, Ray. Oh my gosh, it is so great to see you. How long has it been? Don't answer that, it has been much too long. So, what are you doing now?"

I give my brother a hug, stand back, and say, "Damn, brother, you look good. I guess living in sunny California is your fountain of youth. You do still live there, right?"

"You look good too, Sara," says Ray with a big smile. He does look good, really good, I think, smiling back at him. Does he look better than me? Oh, great, now I am channeling Genevieve. Only she could take a moment like this and turn it around to be just about her.

Jess goes over to Liza and quietly says, "Are you and Ray, like, close? Why didn't he tell us he was coming?"

"No, he just texted me hoping for a ride here, we're friends on Facebook. I figured he told you guys he was coming."

"Okay, I'm opening a lot of wine. Do you happen to know if he has a problem with alcohol, because I think he may have at some point in his life?"

"Jess, open the wine, it's not alcohol. At least that's what Genevieve taught me." Liza is looking towards her grandmother's bedroom, probably wondering if she can hear them all talking.

I sip my wine, watching as Ray takes a glass of Cabernet from Jess and moves away from us. He walks around Genevieve's living room, as if this is the first time he has been here. He picks up framed pictures of my wedding, Parker's wedding, both including Jess. Ray is noticeably missing in those pictures. I think being the baby of this particular family has been hard on Ray. He probably learned at a young age that it was impossible to compete with Jess and Parker. Even as kids they were focused and driven. He didn't need to compete with me—I was neither focused nor driven. But one thing that we had in common that Ray didn't share with us is that Jess, Parker, and I benefited from our grandparents' influence. He didn't spend many summers at their Newport beach house. He was denied those roots that helped keep us somewhat grounded.

Ray takes a big sip of this incredibly delicious Cab and asks, "Where's Genevieve?"

While everyone is milling around in the kitchen, I take the opportunity to sit alone in the living room and enjoy a bit of serenity amidst the chaos that my family has brought to our mother's home. Liza comes over with a half-bottle of Cabernet and sits down next to me.

"More wine?" she asks.

"Sure, you?"

"No, I'll just sip what I have, I have a long drive home. Anyway, Ray and I had quite an interesting conversation on the drive down here."

"That's nice, honey, care to share?" This is actually a really nice Cab.

"Sure, I don't think he'd mind. I don't think much bothers Ray. Mom, he just kind of opened up. He told me that he feels that, out of all of you guys, you and he are the most alike."

"Hmm, that's interesting," I say, wanting to hear more of what Ray said.

"He said that, like you, he did well in school, high grades, which came easy to him. Ray didn't have to apply himself, which is pretty much how he feels he approaches life, a 'why bother' attitude. Ray told me he didn't go to college, same as you, but the difference between you two is that he decided to hitchhike across the country; you got pregnant."

"He did hitchhike, and I did get pregnant, but that was a long time ago. What is the point here, Liza?" I am getting annoyed.

"Mom, please just listen. Ray kept talking. He said he relished the freedom, no one to check in with, other than the short-lived jobs he took to keep some money in his pocket. Most of those jobs were in kitchens or construction, neither of which he liked. He said that he felt like he was on autopilot during those days. He had no passion for anything other than not being tied down. It sounded like he made friends along the way, including a few different girlfriends, but when it was time to take off he said he didn't look back. One interesting thing, though, is that he said that during this trip across the country, he missed the ocean. He said the mountains in Colorado were spectacular; the wilderness in Montana was breathtaking, but nothing compared to what he called his need for water, salty ocean water. Sound familiar, Mom? Anyway, he eventually ended up in Encinitas and got a job in a surf shop. He said the pay sucked, and yes, I know Genevieve hates that word. But I think that this nothing little job opened a big window for Ray."

I am mesmerized by what Liza is saying, and I don't think it's the wine. "So how did this nothing job open windows, Liza?"

Liza quietly continues sharing the conversation that she had with her uncle, my brother.

"Well, Encinitas is a surfing community, actually a pretty well-known surfing community, but according to Ray, it's also a tight-knit surfing community. The surfers weren't exactly welcoming him with open arms. Ray said that they were actually assholes to him. But as luck would have it, Ray met Bobbie Fisher, a surfing god to the locals. Have you ever heard of him? I haven't, but according to Ray, Bobbie has won a lot of surfing competitions around the world. Ray said that when they met, Bobbie was in his fifties, and he had already retired from the professional world of surfing, but still surfed every day. Sounds pretty damn sweet to me, don't you think? Retire from your dream job at age fifty and then get to play in your dream world after that."

I am starting to wonder where I went wrong with Liza—why would she think like that? Oh, wait, she knows that I wish I had found my dream job, made a bunch of money, retired at fifty, and then played for the rest of my life.

"Honey, a bit more wine, please."

"Of course." Liza continues as she pours my wine, "Anyway, Ray said there was an instant connection between the two of them, even though Bobbie was old enough to be his father."

Thank god, Liza is back from wanting to become a fifty-year-old retired surfing champion to realizing that sometimes we grab hold of affection in any shape or form when it shows up in our lives.

"But, Mom, Ray said that Bobbie was kind of like a mentor. Ray was pretty broke, and Bobbie offered him a room at his home. Bobbie took Ray under his wing and taught him how to surf, really surf. Mom, you should have heard Ray talking about surfing. I swear to God, I felt like my car was filling up with amazing energy.

"He talked about learning the basics, talked about how he was embarrassed about having to be taught. You know, kinda like being the twenty-year-old on the Bunny Trail skiing. Anyway, of course, he was like a fish to water. I once told Max and Tess that all of the Austins come from the sea."

"Liza, you said that?"

"I did, Mom. You told me that when I was little. I wanted my kids to know that too."

Deep breath, wow, got one. I did tell that to Liza when she was learning to swim in our unpredictable East Coast ocean, and I am filled with a calm that only the ocean can offer. Liza remembers.

"Back to Ray. He told me Bobbie showed him how to approach a wave, how to dance with a wave, respect the ocean, but also enjoy the ocean, and become one with the ocean. He learned how to embrace his passion, the ocean. So, at this point, Ray is loving life, but still needs to figure out how to pay the bills and love life at the same time."

"Interesting," I say, sipping my wine, hoping my face doesn't show what I'm feeling. What am I feeling, maybe a little jealous of Ray's beach lifestyle? Doesn't matter, I'm exhausted, my feelings don't matter now. "How long has Ray been surfing and how is he making money?"

His talk with my daughter has unnerved me a bit. I should open my eyes to who Ray really is. I should be a better sister, a better person. Right now, I don't have anything extra to give. Sorry, Ray, you are on your own, little gerbil.

That's when our little gerbil interrupts Liza and me.

"Hey, Sara. Liza, can I sit with your mom for a minute?"

Liza gets up, leaving the bottle of wine on the coffee table. She knows me well. Ray sits down next to me, a bit uncomfortably. "Sara, I guess I'm expected to go and see Genevieve, right?"

"Well, only if you want to. But if not, then why are you here, Ray?"

"I don't know. I'm here because I guess I'm supposed to be here. Sara, I can't get a deep breath."

Oh, my god, why do I have to find him a breath? I haven't been able to breathe for weeks.

"Ray, let's do this together. Let's go see Mom."

I can see how uncomfortable my brother is walking into Genevieve's bedroom.

"Mom, there you are," he says, standing away from the bed. I am paralyzed watching Ray, who looks just as paralyzed. "Sara, I can't move my feet; I can't get any further into this room."

I grab Ray. "Shhh, she can hear everything. Just like when we were kids. Watch what you say, Ray."

My brother looks around the room and notices all of the framed photographs on Genevieve's bureaus. These pictures are different than the ones on display for the world to see in the living room. In Genevieve's sanctuary, Ray can see that she has captured his childhood, his grandparents, aunts and uncles, cousins, family friends, his brother and sisters, pictures of him, a history of his life. Genevieve kept a story on her bureau that he probably didn't recall in his mind, but now he's seeing familiar faces, moments frozen in time. He steps closer to the bureau and picks up a black-and-white photo of our mother, young, beautiful, laughing with her four kids playing in the ocean. He moves to another one, Ray all dressed up for the first day of school; in another Ray is posing in his football uniform. Ray is looking at a photo of himself with Parker, Jess, and me, and our family dog. Ray turns to me and quietly says, "We're all smiling, I never noticed the similarity in all of us. We were really a family at some point in my life. Why did I never see these pictures?"

"Who's here?" Genevieve is awake.

I am so used to being in charge I am ready to let Genevieve know that I am there, but Ray turns at that same moment and walks over to her bed.

"Mom, it's me, Ray," he says, taking her hand.

Tears well up in her eyes, slowly roll down her cheeks. In barely a whisper, Genevieve says, "I didn't think you would come, Raymond."

Ray pulls a chair up by her bedside. "Mom, I'm sorry I took so long to come home, but I'm here now, and I'm not going anywhere."

I feel like an intruder, but I am also grateful, intruder or not, to witness my mother and my brother make amends, whatever the hell that means. But I think that Genevieve checked another thing off her to-do-before-I-leave-this-earth list. And I think that Ray is like the rest of us, unsettled, mystified by the impending death of our mother.

Ray leaves Genevieve's side and comes over to me with tears in his eyes. "Thank you," he says to me.

"For what?" I whisper, still acutely aware that Genevieve might be able to hear us.

"For giving me the nudge I needed to come in her room. I realize, although too late, that my running from Mom was not the right way to live my life. I wish I had been stronger, I wish she and I could have talked, I wish that I had accepted her for who she is. I wish for so much. But if I take anything that Mom taught me, it is to never live with regrets. So, no regrets for me, but I am so sad."

"I know, me too," I say as I step close to Ray and hug him tight.

Liza is next. It isn't as if they are waiting in line to see Genevieve, but in a way, it seems like that to me. This is so morbid. "I'm going to go see Genevieve, I'll only be a few minutes," Liza says, walking to Genevieve's bed-room.

Jill and Keith are talking to Ray in the living room—Jess and I are hanging on by a thread in the kitchen. It might as well be Thanksgiving or something. We are all together, just waiting for Genevieve to come out and make her grand entrance.

But it's Liza who comes out of Genevieve's bedroom and quietly shuts the door behind her.

"Liza, are you okay?" Jill asks.

Liza looks sad; sad and perplexed. "Yeah, I'm okay, I just feel...I just feel that Genevieve is unsettled, like she's waiting for someone. I can't shake the feeling I got when I was with her, something just didn't seem right. Who would Genevieve be waiting for?"

"Jess, do you think that she's waiting for Julie or Andrew?" Liza asks, pouring herself a sparkling water. I am sure that at this point, Liza could use a stiff drink.

"I told her they aren't coming for a couple of days and that they both loved her and wished they could be with her. She seemed to understand what I was saying. Although I'm not sure she has another couple of days." She regrets the words as soon as they come out of her mouth.

"Liza, do you want to tell us what happened when you were with Genevieve?" Jill asks.

"Sure, I guess. I'm shocked by how she looks. Genevieve always takes such pride in her looks, but tonight she looks old, incredibly old, and frail. I think that she's barely conscious. She was having difficulty speaking, but she did lift her arms just a bit towards me. I told her how sorry I was, and I took her hand. It was so cold, I pulled the blanket up, tucked it in around her. She was just so cold, that scares me. I talked to her as if we were sitting on her couch, as if we had had too many glasses of wine together, true confessions.

"I said, 'I wish I had come to see you sooner; I'm sorry.' I told her that I really don't have an excuse, other than I was busy, or at least I felt like I was busy. I talked about what I have been doing with work, about the new clients I'm getting. I told her how grateful I am that she pushed me into design, that she gave me the courage to start my own business. And then I said, 'Genevieve, you are the strongest person I have ever known. I have always looked up to you.' I asked her if she remembered when it was 'invite your favorite person to school day' when I was in the first grade and I invited her. Of course, she didn't say anything. I told her that I was so proud to have her as my grandmother, and then told her she was then and still is not your average everyday Grannie. I said, 'You didn't act like my friends' grandmothers, and you sure didn't look like them, especially with the way you dress. You taught me how to stand up for myself, speak my mind, even when it's uncomfortable or not popular. I believe Tess has definitely picked up some of those traits because she sure does speak her mind. You know that Tess thinks that she gets her great fashion style from you. She's probably right.' And then I just sat with her holding her cold hand for a bit longer. I told her that I'll be back tomorrow and said sleep tight. I don't think I said enough."

"You said what's in your heart, Liza. I am sure that Genevieve could hear you, or at the very least, I'm sure she could sense your love for her," I said, getting up to hug Liza. *Genevieve, your family is in pain. We are all hurting, we are stepping into a world without you. That is a testament to your influence on all of us, good or bad.*

Keith quietly goes into his mother-in-law's bedroom, shuts the door, and sits with Genevieve. He tells me later that he was also shocked by her appearance, same as Liza.

"Sara, she looked so vulnerable, it was hard to take in. Genevieve has always been such a force, such a power-house, a ball of energy. I'm really glad that Max didn't see her like this. I want him to remember her as she was. I want him to remember the flamboyant, liberated, vibrant, and alive woman that is his great-grandmother."

Liza decides to leave shortly after, promising to return in the morning. "Goodnight, Mom." We hug and say, "love you." Keith leaves at the same time to make sure Liza is okay to drive. It's pretty obvious that her visit with her grandmother has shaken her.

I watch out the front door as my husband and daughter pull out of the driveway. This is something Genevieve started to do as she got older: watched us leave her and drive away. I shut the door, turn around, and look at my family.

Here we are together, all of us, for Genevieve. We are

coming together as a family, and we are doing it for our mother. No matter the emotional pain we all carry from our parents' unseen neglect we are here for our mother. She has been the anchor that has held this family together. This is a surprising observation to me. I think each of us might feel, as Genevieve would often say, she did the best she could. I think she did do the best that she could for her children.

Jill and Brady are the next to go, leaving the nuclear Austin family to sort things out. It has been years since we were all together.

Parker opens more wine, lots more wine, while we sit at our mother's kitchen table and compare notes.

It doesn't escape me that Genevieve is just a few feet away, in her bedroom, dying. She is freaking dying, and we are sitting out here drinking. As a family and individually we do drink a lot. None of us seem the least bit concerned that we do this, drink a lot. I think it might be because our measuring stick for consuming too much alcohol was our father and he puts us to shame in this category.

Who had it worst growing up, who had it best, good memories, bad memories, whatever we felt like sharing with each other, we shared. Surprisingly, we were quite candid and open, probably due to the wine.

Parker points his wine glass at Jess and says, "Remember when you got suspended from school and Genevieve showed up in her big fur hat and red leather coat?"

"I still have nightmares about that. Why couldn't she have just come in a sensible winter coat and a normal hat like every other mother? Why did she always have to stand out? I was so embarrassed. But in retrospect, that was a damn nice outfit," says Jess, sipping her wine.

Ray and I are laughing at Jessica, and then she looks at me.

"Oh Sara, Sara, Sara. You shouldn't be laughing so much. I am quite sure that you remember the night you got caught sneaking out, or should I say sneaking in?"

"Oh, just shut up, Jess," was my feeble attempt at a comeback.

"No, seriously, what happened? I don't remember this," Ray says.

"Well, Raymond, my dear brother, let me jog your memory," Jess says while smirking at me. "Sara who never did anything wrong."

"You mean Sara who never got caught doing anything wrong," interrupts Parker.

"Okay, Sara who never got caught. But Sara did get caught and it was big, and it was good." Jessica is really getting into reliving her little story.

"Jess, just tell the story," says Ray. I'm thinking Ray seems awfully eager to hear about me getting in trouble.

"It was in early June before we went to Meme and Pops for the summer. Sara was about fourteen, I think. Anyway, she snuck out of the house after Genevieve had gone to bed. Not that Genevieve ever came in to say goodnight and tuck us in. But that's another story. Anyway, I had just come home, right at curfew, and went to bed. I heard someone walking down the hall and then I heard the back door open. I looked out my window and there was Sara, sneaking out of the house. I have to say that I was surprised and somewhat proud that my little sister had the guts to do what she was doing."

"So, what happened?" asked Ray.

"Well, I tried to stay awake, but I couldn't. Around four o'clock in the morning, I heard voices—well, Genevieve's voice. I'm not sure how she knew it, but Genevieve was waiting in Sara's bedroom when Sara snuck back in. I mean, seriously, who gets caught sneaking back in?" Jessica says, laughing, which only got Ray and Parker laughing. I wasn't laughing, I was glaring at all three of them.

"Damn, Sara, and you have lived to tell the tale. How did you get out of that one?" asks Ray.

Big sigh. "I didn't get out of it. I mean, how could I lie my way out of it? It's four in the morning and I'm sneaking back to my bedroom after being out all night."

"Come on, Sara, there's got to be more to this story," pipes up Parker.

"Okay, okay. So, I opened my door as quietly as possible and go into the room. I don't even turn on the light. And that's when I heard, 'Where the hell have you been, Sara?' I just about jumped out of my skin, I was so surprised, actually stunned. And then I realized it was Genevieve. She turned on the light, shot me a look of disgust, and walked out of the room. Right before she slammed my door shut, Genevieve turned around, pointed her finger at me, and said, 'Don't ever pull another stunt like this, Sara Austin. Or it will be your last stunt.' Okay, you guys, let's pick on someone else. Oh, I have one. Ray, remember when Parker was babysitting you and you broke your toe?"

Now it's Ray's turn to glare at us. "I sure do remember that. My toe still aches when it rains."

"Then it's a good thing you live in Southern Cal, little brother," Parker says.

"Yeah, but the worst part was that Parker swore me to secrecy, to not tell anyone or he would have gotten in big trouble with Genevieve."

"What exactly happened, Parker?" I am enjoying this.

"It's not really a big deal," says Parker.

"Not a big deal? Dude, you broke my fucking toe."

"I didn't break your toe; you broke your toe."

"Come on, Parker, spill." Seems Jessica is enjoying this tale as well.

"Alright. I was watching Ray, who was a pain in the ass then and it seems to me that he still is. Anyway, he was driving me crazy, so I told him to go out and play. I mean it's not like I was sending him out to play on city streets, it was our backyard. I don't know how long he was out there, maybe a while, but I figured I should check on him. At first, I didn't see him, but then there he was lying on the ground next to that garden bench we used to have. Do you guys remember that bench? He was crying, crying so hard that he couldn't talk. I didn't know what the hell had happened. I got Ray to calm down, and then I noticed the bench was tipped over. That was a really heavy wrought-iron bench. Ray told me he was trying to walk on the top of the back-rest, like a tightrope walker in the circus. Well, the bench fell over, with Ray, and it landed on his foot. That's where he was hurt. I took off his sneaker, looked at his foot, and figured out he had only broken his pinky toe. My boy-scout training sprang into action."

We all moaned at this point. "Come on, Parker."

"I helped him hobble back to the house and put some ice on it. Ray was crying, saying even the ice hurt. Genevieve was going to be home in about an hour, and I needed to figure something out fast."

"Go on," says Jess.

"I remembered that Jimmy Martin's mom was a nurse. You guys remember Jimmy, right? Anyway, I told him to tell his mom he was doing a paper for his biology class, and that he wanted to know what to do for a broken pinky toe."

"Oh, my god, Parker, how devious and brilliant of you." I never knew this side of Parker.

"Jimmy called back and said that his mom first asked why was he asking these questions, did he break his toe? She bought the paper story and told him you really can't do anything for a broken pinky, it will heal on its own. You should apply ice and try to stay off it. I told Ray that it was going to be fine. That I had talked to a nurse and she said we shouldn't tell Mom or any adult."

Jess and I just look at each other, mouths wide open.

"Ray believed me, he never told anyone, but I guess the traitor told you two," Parker says, pointing at Jess and me. "And Genevieve never found out. End of story."

"Okay, Raymond, time for you to share your best or worst—however you want to look at it—Genevieve story," Parker says, looking at his brother.

Ray is quiet for a minute; I'm thinking he must have so many that he's trying to figure out which is the best story.

Ray takes a sip of wine and says, "Actually, I don't have a story to tell."

"Oh, come on," Jess, Parker, and I say at the same time.

"Ray, you have to have something. Come on, play nice, we all shared and humiliated ourselves." Jess is not going to let him slide on this one.

"No, really, you guys, I have nothing. By the time I was old enough to do crazy things, things that could get me in trouble with Genevieve, she had stopped caring, at least about me. I'm not sure if she actually ever did care. Trust me, I did my fair share of stupid kid stuff, and if Genevieve did find out about it, she just ignored it. I was pretty much a free-range kid."

The four of us go quiet. I think we must all be digesting the stories we just heard. For me, it's Ray's non-story; that's the sad one.

I get up to open another bottle of wine, turn around to my siblings, and say, "Sounds like we were not the easiest kids in the world. Jeez, maybe we are the reason Genevieve is the way she is. Maybe we pushed her over the edge. Who wants Pinot or Chardonnay?"

After a bit more wine I bring down boxes of photos, old report cards, handmade cards we had made as kids. I discovered them in the guestroom closet while wearing my wedding dress.

We are all really surprised that Genevieve has kept all of these memorabilia. I find a card I had made for Genevieve when I was probably about five years old. The artwork was indicative, even then, that I would never be an artist. But in red and blue crayon I told my mother that I loved her and that she was the best mother anyone could have. This little card confused me—was there a time that I actually felt that? Was there a time that Genevieve was a warm, nurturing 'mommy?' Not that I can recall. I pour everyone more wine and say goodnight, taking my glass up to the guest room. Parker and Jess are doing the doses tonight and it was decided that one of them would sleep in

Genevieve's room, in the chair right next to her bed, so that she isn't alone. I'm taking the six a.m. shift; Ray isn't included in this schedule. Some things never change.

WINTER DAY

"It wasn't raining when Noah built the ark."
– Howard Rugg

I lie in bed, exhausted, but I can't fall asleep.

I can hear Jess, Ray, and Parker talking and drinking until it's time for the midnight doping. Can Genevieve hear them as well? If so, I would think that this would make her feel happy, knowing that her family is here for her—as long as she can't actually hear what they're saying. Jess has the midnight to three a.m. shift with Genevieve. I wonder how long it will be before she's asleep sitting in Genevieve's bedside chair.

I start thinking about Jess. I wonder how she's really doing with all of this.

Jessica has had a very rocky relationship with Genevieve, just like the rest of us, but also different than each of us.

I am well aware that Jess never felt that she could never measure up in our mother's eyes. She tried so hard to please her, and for years she didn't understand why her own mother didn't love her. As a young child, then adolescent, Jess didn't realize Genevieve loved only one person and that was herself. Growing up with parents who are

208

pathologically disconnected from their children seeps deep into one's soul, to stew and fester well into adulthood. For my sister, she felt that the only time that she got any attention was when she got caught acting out. Then Genevieve showed her the attention Jess craved, but it wasn't love or concern, but anger—nothing physical, but emotionally destructive. Jess's best memories, like mine, aren't of either of our parents, but of our grandparents. Jess loved to cook with Meme and Meme loved to pass on her recipes and skills to her oldest grandchild. From our grandfather, Pops, she learned what it meant to be the center of attention, in a good way. The summers with our grandparents kept Jess afloat; they kept her from drowning.

Genevieve was something of a Jekyll and Hyde. Even though she showed us little motherly love, making us think that she didn't care, she also kept us in line, or thought she did, with unreasonable rules. Jess was the first to test Genevieve's boundaries, refusing to stick to unrealistic curfews, going to parties that were off-limits, and perfecting the art of working around Genevieve. Jess and Genevieve's battles came to a head when Jess was about seventeen. She was done with our mother's unreasonableness and went to live with our alcoholic father in his small two-bedroom apartment over a pizza joint. I remember at the time thinking sadly that that was preferable to staying at home. And even more sadly—I was still in that home.

Jess spent that summer with Dad, who seemed to be trying to do his best to stay sober, but she told me that she was always on edge. "Am I going to get a call that he's been in an accident, he's killed someone, or worse, he's dead?"

She started college in the fall, as far away from our

family as she could get. In her first semester as a freshman at Stanford, she met Brad, a sophomore studying law. He was different from any of the other guys that she had dated; he was more mature, athletic, adventurous. They married two summers later and moved into an apartment, starting their life together. It was a small wedding, immediate family only. She told me that she was beyond happy. She went to classes, did well in school, baked some of Meme's wonderful sweets, and loved making dinner every night. She and Brad played tennis, hiked on weekends. Life was good. Life was so different from before. "I am pretty sure this is how a normal family acts," she said during one of our rare phone calls.

Jess was ecstatic when she found out she was pregnant; it was her chance to be everything our mother wasn't. Brad was not quite as ecstatic as my sister. He was worried. They were so young, how could they support a child with both of them still in school? Genevieve was also not quite as ecstatic as her daughter. How dare she make her a grandmother?

Julie was born shortly after Brad graduated. He joined his father's law firm and their little family moved to Washington, DC, to begin the next chapter of their life together.

Fast-forward to the following year. Jess, Brad, and Julie welcomed baby Andrew to the family. Once again, my sister was over the moon. She eventually went back to school, working towards her nursing degree. The original plan was to go to grad school and get a degree in child behavior, but two children and one income put that plan on the back burner.

Their life was hectic as it would be for any young

family with a lot of balls in the air, but they were making it work. Things got easier once the kids entered public schools—no more juggling childcare for Brad and Jess.

Genevieve would visit on occasion and Jess tried, for her kids' sake, to keep their grandmother in their lives. She made sure to spend either Thanksgiving or Christmas with Genevieve, even if that meant the expense of four train tickets to Bridgeport, Connecticut, and shipping the gifts from Santa ahead of time to Parker, who would be sure to get them under Genevieve's tree for Christmas morning. By this time, our grandparents had sold the big, beautiful summer house, downsized to a smaller home closer to town, rather than the beach, and wintered in Florida. Jess told me she was sad that her kids would never experience the joy and freedom on the shores of Newport, Rhode Island as we had.

Brad's family's law firm was expanding, and he was offered the opportunity to open up a new office in Scottsdale, Arizona. Since it was Brad's father doing the offering, Brad had few options, other than to say yes. Jess and Brad flew out to Scottsdale and bought a Mediterranean-style home, in a good school district, with four bedrooms and a pool after three days of house-hunting. Within six weeks of accepting the offer to relocate, Jess had her family settled into their new home and their new life. We spoke occasionally during this time and she was always upbeat—weather was great, the kids loved school, the neighbors were so friendly, not at all like us New Englanders. Her only source of concern was how much Brad was working and the pressure he was putting on himself. She thought about going back to school to finish working toward her nursing degree, but felt it was more important to try to keep things stable at home for both the kids and Brad.

Three years after their move across the country, Brad dropped dead of a heart attack while presenting a case in court. Jessica collapsed, emotionally and physically. This was such a shock and she told me later that she wasn't sure she would be able to keep going—her kids were what saved her. We all went to Brad's funeral and tried to do what was best for Jess, but truthfully Parker, Ray, and I were useless. Brad's parents stayed with Jess and the kids for a few weeks. They helped with the meals, the children, the day-to-day routine, allowing her to grieve and hopefully get stronger, but they couldn't stay forever. They also needed to grieve for their son but felt it important that their grandchildren were a priority. We can grieve when we go home, they had said to Jess.

Genevieve arrived the day they were departing, but would stay for only for a week, maybe two at the most. However, in true Genevieve form, she wanted to be waited on, treated like a queen, and get out and do things. "It will be good for you to get back to your old self, or better yet a new and improved version of that," Genevieve had told Jess.

So Jess did what she does best—pulled herself together, stood up, brushed off the pain, sadness, despair, and rejoined the human rat race. I had wondered then if it was to get Genevieve out of her house and off her back. Whatever it was, it seemed to work.

While Julie and Andrew were in school, Jess returned to nursing school part-time, got a job at a nearby hospital, and eventually got her degree.

Time moved on for all of us. Julie and Andrew graduated high school and went on to graduate from college. They both headed out to take on the world, making their mother proud.

Jess's career flourished. She had continued with her education, eventually getting her RN degree. She moved up the ladder, ultimately becoming the chief nurse at the Scottsdale Shea Medical Center Pediatric Ward. But something was still missing—a partner to share her life with. As fate would have it, she met Russ Richardson, a successful publisher, at an art opening. They hit it off while standing in front of Maxfield Parrish's Grand Canyon painting. They soon discovered they were kindred spirits and married six months after meeting. For Jess, a door opened, and she stepped into a brand-new world.

Although Jess and Genevieve seemed to always be at odds, Jess continuously made a valiant attempt to keep our mother happy and to keep the hurt Genevieve inflicted on her to herself. Jess would initiate calls to Genevieve to keep the communication open. Jess and Genevieve would travel together. They would meet in New York for shows and dinner, museums, art galleries. They had a lot in common. These trips would stress Jess out, trying to be sure that everything was perfect, but she did it time and time again. One time she said to me, "I know that you think I'm a glutton for punishment, but it's the right thing to do." And that summed up Jessica Austin, who always tried to do the right thing. I, on the other hand, did everything I could to avoid spending time with my mother—hence my fondness for outgoing tides.

It's three a.m. I hear Parker get up and go downstairs. Now it's his turn. I hear Jess slowly come up the stairs and shut the door to the other guest room. This house exudes weariness.

I know that Parker is giving Genevieve her dose of morphine and I can only imagine that he is wondering what the hell is he doing.

But in true Parker form, I hear him put soothing music on his phone to play for Genevieve as he settles in for three hours to sit with his mother. I toss and turn; sleep is not my friend.

I come down for the six a.m. shift, fill up the syringe right to the line where it's supposed to be, and go to the bedroom to help our mother on her way.

"Parker, I think the toilet is running, do you hear water?" I whisper.

"That's the music I have been playing for her, it's soothing."

"Yeah, well, all that sound of running water makes me need to pee."

For an instant, Parker and I share a laugh. We are in a good place with each other. I wonder if Genevieve can hear us. I hope so. I want her to know that all is well with her kids.

"How is she?" I ask after squirting the poison in her mouth.

"Quiet, she's been quiet. I'm going to bed. Good luck."

I sit on the side of Genevieve's bed. The birds are just starting to chirp, and I notice a yellow legal pad on her bureau. What's this, I wonder. I don't remember it being here before, I think as I pick it up. That's because it has never been there. This is Parker's scribble; he must have been writing while sitting here. I shouldn't read it, but it looks like a letter to Genevieve. Screw it, I am reading it. I get up, make sure her door is shut tight, and settle back into the world's most uncomfortable chair. This chair is definitely for looks, not function.

Genevieve, I hope that you can read this, but if you can't then I will read it to you. This is not easy for me. You and I haven't been on the same page for what seems like a long time. I used to be able to talk to you, share things, always able to take your comments with a grain of salt. Something changed for me over the last few years; maybe things changed for me when I became a father. I don't know, but I do know that you don't have a lot of time left and this isn't how I want things to end for you and me. There is so much I want to ask you, so much I want to hear from you. I think an apology from you would be a great place to start. And then an explanation, why are you the way you are? I have always heard how people regret leaving things unsaid until it's too late. I'm afraid this is the case for you and me. I want you to know that I may never understand who you really are, but you are my mother, for good or bad, and I will always be a little conflicted about my feelings for you. But in the end I do admire who you are and love you.

Holy shit, I think, putting down the letter. I feel sorry for Parker, and at the same time, I feel protective of Genevieve. I also wish I hadn't read this.

I put the legal pad back where it was, turn on some soothing meditation music, and watch Genevieve's chest move up and down. She seems to be in a deep sleep. I need to stay awake, and Parker's letter is doing the job for me. Damn, we all have some baggage.

I think back to when my brother was a senior at Brown. He and a few of his buddies were spending spring break skiing, snowboarding, and doing all the typical things that young men do during spring break. But these guys chose the mountains over the islands: Jackson Hole, Wyoming. Ironically, Jill, then a senior from Yale, was doing the same thing with a few of her friends, avoiding the cluster that is spring break on basically any beach at that time of year. That's where he and Jill met.

Parker had opted out of taking on the mountain and decided instead to join in a friendly game of ultimate snow Frisbee. It turned out that most of the players were a group from Southern California, dudes who take their Frisbee seriously. One player was knocked out of the game with a bloody nose. As Parker tells the story, that's when, out of nowhere, a petite coed jumped in to take over for the injured guy and threw a sidearm toss right into the hands of a guy in the end zone, for the goal.

Parker was a goner. Any girl that could care less about playing in the snow with this crazy group of guys and who could throw a Frisbee like she could—well, the rest is history. They were practically inseparable for the rest of spring break. They realized that they had a lot in common. They both were driven to succeed in anything they took on in life and they both enjoyed a challenge. Parker and Jill decided they were right for each other. It was a decision they made together, no surprises for this couple, not a down-on-one-knee-in-a-restaurant type of couple. They were a team. They married two years later and formed a dynamic partnership as both a married couple and business partners. Parker seemed genuinely happy. Their business was flourishing and he really loved Jill. They are best friends and they included Genevieve as much as possible in their lives. The three of them went out to dinner, traveled together...life was good. Jill and Parker's focus for years was on each other and their business. They had decided to hold off on starting a family and concentrate on growing their business for the future. Time got the better of them as they sold one business and launched another startup. However, once they were sure of their commercial success, they realized the clock was ticking away—time to start a family. A few years later their son was born, and Parker's world turned upside down. At first, he didn't know what to do with this tiny person, but after weeks of no sleep, walking the floor, taking Brady for two a.m. car rides to put him to sleep, and endless diaper changes, Parker was struck by the emotions that his child stirred in him. Parker had told me that he felt protective of Brady. He wanted to shield him from the big, bad world, and he was going to do everything in his power to be the best parent that he could be.

Now he would lead by example. This is what a father does, this is what a father is like, this is how a father loves his son.

I have watched my brother be a parent, and he is one of the good ones. Once again, he and Jill have formed another successful partnership; this one is named parenting.

Jess is up early. She makes coffee for us and we sit quietly with our mother. Together we do the nine a.m. doping. Both of us are now experts at administering morphine. Genevieve seems a bit agitated this morning. Maybe that's a good sign, maybe it means she's coming around, maybe it means we have longer with her than Hospice Mary said. I could probably use some of this morphine, I think.

I say nothing to Jess about Parker's letter to Genevieve.

I don't think that she would judge me for reading it, but I do feel that I invaded his private thoughts, and have decided to leave them as just that, my brother's private thoughts. This is between Parker and Genevieve, and neither of them needs any interference or advice from Jess or me. The funny thing—or not so funny thing—about what Parker revealed in the letter is something that I think we all—Jess, Ray, and I—have felt many times. Why are you the way you are, Genevieve? In an effort to maintain our sanity and still have a relationship with our mother, we have each drifted out with a tide, and we are the ones who choose when or even if we will float back in.

The house is peaceful. Ray and Parker are upstairs sleeping. Liza arrived earlier this morning, She and Jess are out for a walk. Tess is working, and Max is home with his dad. Jill and Brady are due to arrive later today. It's a beautiful but cold winter day; the sun is streaming into the house. All I hear is the clock ticking and an extremely loud and annoying red cardinal sitting in a tree outside the kitchen window. I swear that bird is looking right at me and squawking. Wonder if this red cardinal is a spirit who has come to visit? I should probably check on Genevieve.

Her breathing has calmed down. Genevieve seems more relaxed than earlier this morning. Everything is so quiet. I sit with my mother, not saying anything. I feel that she can sense that I'm here, just the tiniest bit. I think I may have missed the chance to ask my mother so many questions that I never had the nerve to ask. And if I did ask her now, if she could talk to me, would her answers be riddled with disdain, would she still take me down if I asked her a question from my heart? Then I notice a change in her. Genevieve's breathing has slowed down, her eyes open. I'm excited. "Mom, hi, it's me, Sara, but of course you know that." I'm stumbling over my words.

Genevieve takes a gulp of air.

"Mom, are you okay?" I ask. Now I'm kind of scared but I don't know why.

Genevieve has a smile on her face. She speaks so quietly I need to get closer to her to hear. "What are you saying, Mom?"

"You are here, you came, you have the boat for us to sail away in. I have the courage now. Give me your hand, I have been waiting for you, Nicholas, my baby boy."

"Mom." I watch as my mother gasps for her last breath of air. At that second, at that last breath, my mother is dead. I react strangely. I stand up, looking at the skylight, the ceiling, and ask out loud, "Are you here, are you still here? Mom, are you here?" It's as if I am expecting to see her floating off to heaven. Oh my god, I need her to be here. I need a sign, a goodbye, Mom, anything instead of just leaving your body, leaving me, leaving me all alone. Mom?

"Oh my god, what do I do? Mom, oh no, what do I do?" I don't know why, but I can't leave her alone. I don't want to yell to wake up my brothers. I can't text anyone because my phone is in the other room, so I sit in silence alone with my mother. I just sit with my dead mother. In silence, alone, with my dead mother. Did she really say what I think she did? Nicholas, my baby boy? I absolutely cannot breathe at this moment.

I look at my mother, who looks as if she is asleep, not dead. "Mom, I know you aren't here. I want to thank you for letting me be a part of your journey. You did it with dignity and grace. As usual, Genevieve, you did it your way." I just sit. I just sit.

I hear the front door open and know that it must be Liza and Jess; Slowly I get up from Genevieve's side and go to the foyer. Liza comes in first, Jess right behind her. Liza looks at me. I just stand there, looking at my daughter. I have no words, but the mantle has been passed, another generation of Austin mothers and daughters sharing a look that will stay with each of us to the end of time.

Liza comes toward me with an all-knowing look on her face. "Mom?"

Jess looks up towards me. She has stopped in her tracks. "Sara, what's wrong?"

"She's gone. Genevieve is gone."

Jess, Liza, and I go into Genevieve's bedroom. Liza has tears rolling down her face. I hear her whisper, "Oh, Genevieve, I don't want you to be gone. Rest in peace, my amazing Genevieve, I will always love you," as she bends down to kiss her grandmother goodbye. Jess just stands there, not a word, she just stands next to her mother's bed.

I leave them with Genevieve and go upstairs to wake up Parker and Ray. First, I lightly shake Parker, who is dead to the world. Poor choice of words again.

"Hey, wake up, Parker, you need to wake up."

Ray hears me and gets up and comes into the guest bedroom.

"Leave me alone, Sara. I'm trying to sleep." Parker is grouchy.

"What's going on, Sara?" Ray asks with a big yawn.

My internal reaction is "screw you both, wake the fuck up, and listen to me." But instead, I gently tell my brothers that our mother—their mother—I tell them that Genevieve died just a few minutes ago.

Parker jumps out of bed. "Seriously, she's dead?" he asks.

No, Parker, April Fools, this is all just a big, horrible joke.

"How do you know, Sara, are you sure?" Ray asks as we both watch Parker struggling to get into his straight-legged Burberry pants.

"I'm pretty damn sure; I was with her. I was sitting with Mom when she took her last breath."

Parker and Ray go downstairs into the master bedroom and stand with Jess and Liza and dead Genevieve.

Keith arrives a few minutes later, just as he had planned. What Keith didn't plan on was Genevieve leaving us quite so soon. None of us did.

I'm sipping a cup of tea watching Liza walk around her grandmother's home, quietly, alone, almost reverently looking at objects around the house, not touching, just breathing in the essence of her grandmother. Calls have been made. Genevieve's friends and neighbors are coming in to pay their respects, yet Liza moves quietly alone among them.

She looks up and sees me watching her. "Happy birthday, Mom."

I smile at my beautiful daughter. "Thanks, Liza, not a big deal."

All of a sudden, the Austins come together. Parker gives me an awkward hug and jokes, "Well, I guess nobody is going to forget your birthday now, unless of course we forget when Genevieve died."

Ray whispers in my ear, "Some things never change, happy birthday, Sara."

The standing joke, not a joke to me, is that nobody

really knows what my actual birthdate is. Genevieve had manipulated it to the point that my father and grand-parents were never quite sure. February was an in-convenient time for children's birthday parties as far as Genevieve was concerned. February was the perfect time to be in the South of France. So my family celebrated my birthday at the whim of Genevieve, which became the family joke.

Jess walks over to me, quietly, and opens her hands. She is holding Genevieve's favorite necklace, the one she was wearing when she died. Not a word is spoken. Jess hands me the necklace and looks deep into my eyes. Another bond is formed, sister to sister, one that will never be broken. I put on the necklace. I touch it, feel it sitting on my collarbone. Is there any sense of Genevieve still attached to this necklace? I'm not sure, but I do feel somehow connected to her wearing it.

It's after seven p.m. We are all sitting at the dining-room table, exhausted, shell-shocked. Today at twelve-twenty-five p.m., we lost our mother, our matriarch, and, surprisingly, our anchor. Even though we all knew this would happen, we are each struggling to wrap our brains around it.

Jess had taken out the binder Hospice Mary had left and started on the "What to do when your loved one passes on" list.

She called hospice and let them know that Genevieve had passed. Hospice Mary was there within thirty min-utes. The crematorium was called and instructed when to pick up Genevieve. Since it was the weekend the other calls could wait. It felt as if the energy of Genevieve's home had left with her. There was nothing left here.

I alone had witnessed my mother's last breath. But we were together, as a family, when the undertakers took her body out to the hearse.

We, as a family, all blindly accepted the condolences of the neighbors. We sat with Emma and our cousins, drinking tea, not knowing what to say or how to act.

Liza left shortly after her grandmother's body was removed, taking Ray with her. He had already looked into flights back home, to his home. Parker, Brady, and Jill stayed until everyone had left, and Keith left shortly after that.

"You sure you don't want to come home tonight?" he quietly asked me.

"I don't see how I can leave Jess here alone. It's just too eerie, surreal. We need to make some final arrangements, get the rental company to come and get the bed and the other stuff we rented. I will be home tomorrow, I promise."

Jess is heating up the chicken soup, although neither of us are hungry. I open up wine.

"What the hell are we going to do with all this morphine? Save for a what-if situation? Does morphine have a shelf life?" I ask, not sure if Jess is even listening.

"Look in the binder, it tells you how to dispose of it. Unless of course you want to bring all of that home."

"Did we kill her?" I whisper these words, afraid to say them too loud, afraid of what Jess was going to say.

"No, we didn't kill her. Mom didn't want to linger. She made that clear. We did what we were supposed to do. We did what Genevieve wanted."

"But it happened so quickly—think about it. Less than three weeks ago, she went into the hospital—I spent nine days in there with her, never thinking that she was going to die. Here we are seventeen days later and Mom is dead. I mean, did we give her too much?"

"I agree, she went much faster than anticipated, but Sara, we did what we were told. Mom wanted to die, she did, end of story. How's the soup?"

"Not bad considering I don't like chicken soup."

BREATHE

"Promise me you'll always remember: You're braver than
you believe and stronger than you seem,
and smarter than you think."
– Carter Crocker

T hree months to the day after Genevieve Austin's
death, her family comes together one more time. We
are celebrating her life.

We are all there. Jess and Russ. Julie and Andrew, their
spouses, and their children. Keith and I, along with Liza,
her husband Sam, Max, and Tess. Parker, Jill, and Brady.
Ray and Bobbie. Ray had decided it was time for Bobbie to
meet the family and for the family to meet Bobbie.

We gather at our mother's grave, just the Austins and
our Aunt Emma. Genevieve's side of the headstone has a
lovely piece of AstroTurf, courtesy of Parker. He knew that
it would be thrown out after we left, but this was a gesture
of love from Parker to his mother. I brought a beautiful
bouquet of calla lilies, one for each of us. Calla lilies were
Genevieve's favorite. It's funny that she always loved
them, considering that calla lilies were her wedding bouquet and Genevieve always seemed to hate everything that
had to do with her relationship with our father. Genevieve

will always be an enigma to me. Jess made sure there was enough champagne and glasses for all. She even brought sparkling cider for the kids. No detail was left undone.

Each person speaks, just a few words about their mother, mother-in-law, grandmother, great-grandmother. Jess, Parker, Ray, and I are stiff with our words. I feel awkward speaking about Genevieve; it isn't comfortable or easy for any of her children to do this.

All of the others, however, through tears, speak eloquently about the impact Genevieve had on their life. Each grandchild speaks from the heart—how Genevieve made each feel special, loved, each believing they were her favorite. Genevieve made a powerful impression on her grandchildren, and this completely dumbfounded the four of us, her own children. After each person speaks, they put their calla lily on the AstroTurf. I think that Genevieve would have liked that little touch. We hold our glasses in the air.

"To Genevieve," Keith says.

"To Genevieve."

I'm not sure why these two words are touching my heart. I finish my champagne, fight back tears, pour another glass, and leave it on my mother's grave. To Mom, I whisper.

After the memorial, our little group returns to Genevieve's home and welcomes all of the people from the list that she had given me while in the hospital. Parker had followed our mother's wishes and personally called each person to let them know she had passed. Parker told me that one thing that struck him was how loved and admired Genevieve was. For an instant, he said he wished there was a way to rewind, redo his life. Try to get to know her better.

Per Genevieve's orders, the food is tasteful, the wine white, and the tributes to her numerous. Our mother was loved, admired, and respected by so many. Once again, her children, the four of us, are taken by surprise. After all, didn't we know her the best?

"Sara, let's get out of here, just us. Let's go for a walk," Jess says. We slip out the front door. I sense Jess doesn't want anyone interrupting us. We have each tucked a beer in our coat pockets and walk in silence until we come to the park. We sit on a bench and open our beers.

Ping, it's my cell ringing. I look at the caller ID and don't answer.

"Do you need to get that?"

"Nope, it's work. I hand in my resignation Monday. Since losing Mom I have taken a step back, or more accurately, a step inward," I say while actually taking a deep breath.

"I'm not sure what you mean, a step inward," says Jess, giving me an odd look.

"I've learned so much and have felt so many emotions during my nine days with Mom in the hospital, I don't want to lose that momentum. I've kept my real emotions at bay for probably most of my life. Now I've shifted those emotions to something better, something positive. For the last few months, I have been focusing on forgiveness, compassion, and healing myself. I can now say, with confidence, that I am a person who is worthy of being recognized for her strengths, her positive contributions to those around her. I have started to listen to my heart, lead with my heart, and stay focused on all of the gifts that I have in my life. I no longer need to be with people who don't value me. Honestly, I don't think that I have ever known what I want from life and now I finally realize that what I want is what I have. My circumstances don't dictate my reality. Coming out from under Genevieve's thumb, leaving my job—that's just part of who I am. I'm comfortable in my own skin, same skin I was born with. Only took sixty-odd years to figure that out."

"Wow, Sara, that's a huge step, submitting your resignation. Good for you. As Pops would say, you done good, kid. I'm not sure what all the other stuff means, but if you feel good, then so be it."

"Thanks, it feels good. I feel good, I feel confident, secure, and lighter. But judging from your need to talk to me alone, I sense that I won't be feeling quite so good in a minute."

"I'm sorry, really I don't want to squash your good mood, but I need to tell you something."

Another sip of beer for me, just to steel my nerves for whatever it is my sister has to say.

"The kids want to put together a book about Genevieve's life. They want to use her photos, memories from her life, interview people who knew her, that kind of stuff," Jess says.

"It's kinda late for that. Genevieve took her memories with her," I say, and then take a large swig of my beer. I probably should have brought a couple of beers.

"I know that, but they think this would be a tribute to her memory, to our family for generations to come. They're excited that there's so many photos, cards, letters, memorabilia, even her mortgage payoff statement, she threw nothing out." My sister takes an equally large swig of her beer.

"Okay, but that means they might be opening up some doors that should be left closed. I'm worried, especially as you said, she threw nothing out. We should have been upfront from the beginning."

"How? How would we have done that? Sit each of our kids down at a planned age and explain the past to them? At what age would that have been acceptable? What would have been the reason for all of that confusion, pain, hurt? They would have questions. And we don't have the answers. Only Genevieve has those answers, and those went to the grave with her." Jess is close to hyperventilating, and I can feel my blood pressure heading for the roof. I thought that all of this, everything connected to Genevieve, was behind us. So much for my Zen attitude.

"Sara, I've done a lot of research on Ancestry and found nothing. There isn't anything that can be linked to our family. The records are closed. So, we tell them they can do that. They can make the book. In the meantime, you and I start going through every single piece of paper that Mom left to make sure things line up."

"Damn it, I really want this to all go away. I want to go away."

"I know you do, Sara, but not just yet, please."

"Don't worry, that's the old Sara talking. I'm not going away. We can face any challenges as long as we stick together as Genevieve's kids."

EPILOGUE
ONE YEAR LATER

"Change is the law of life, and those who look only to the past and the present are certain to miss the future."
– John F. Kennedy

R ay gets up early just like he has every day for the last year. He brings Bobbie a cup of coffee, gives him a kiss and an "I love you." Then Ray checks the weather, the surf, the tides, and heads off to open the surf shop. He feels different, looks different than a year ago. Ray feels good, feels grateful. He has turned his life around. Genevieve's death has given Ray a new outlook on life. He stopped partying and drinking, choosing instead to focus on his future. Ray and Bobbie pooled their money and bought a surf shop, which is starting to make a profit. For some reason today he is thinking of his mother—that hasn't happened in a while. Ray steps out into the sunshine, looks up, and smiles. Thanks, Mom.

Jessica adjusts her seatbelt and settles into her first-class seat for the long flight to Japan. Russ is next to her organizing his books on tape, newspapers, and magazines. As the Boeing 747 leaves the runway, charges up through the clouds into the sunshine, Jess thinks of her mother. She knows it has been exactly one year since Genevieve passed. With sadness and love, Jess looks out her window, sips her champagne, and whispers, "Love you, Mom."

Parker showers after a run on the beach, then sits down in his home office and starts typing. He is about six chapters into a novel he's writing, and he can't stop. Parker hasn't been this energized in a long time. He is struggling with the title, but it might simply be, *A Woman Called Genevieve*. A bright red cardinal lands on his windowsill, and Parker stops typing, takes in the significance of this. *Thanks, Mom.*

"Hello?"

"Happy birthday."

"Oh, thanks for remembering."

"Of course I remembered. How are you?"

"I miss Genevieve today, probably because she passed a year ago today. It's odd, I feel sad and grateful at the same time. I'm so grateful that I had those nine days to be with her in the hospital. I think of those days as precious, something I will never forget."

"I'm sorry you're sad, but it's nice that you are. It means you deeply miss her. She left you with a feeling of love for her and that's a gift, just like your nine days with her. It's okay to be sad, but not for too long. Genevieve wouldn't tolerate much melancholy or mushy stuff, not then, not now."

"Spoken like a true Austin, my darling Liza."

"Madame? I believed you ordered a Grey Goose martini straight up, rocks on the side with a twist?"

"Yes, I did."

"Happy birthday, baby."

Sara smiles at her husband as he hands her the drink. She looks out to the ocean from the deck of their new winter home on Captiva Island, watching the tide come in. She no longer looks for an outgoing tide. Sara is peaceful and calm. Sara can breathe. Life is good. *Thank you, Mom.*

THE
END